BOOK

Within the shadowy recesses of Collins House, Victoria Winters helps Elizabeth Stoddard open a secret room in preparation for the arrival of elderly Henry Collins.

From the first meeting with the mysterious old man, Victoria senses that he holds a vital key to her past. When he makes her a secret present of the magnificent jewels which belonged to the woman he loved—a woman Victoria strongly resembles—she is sure she is on the verge of discovering her real identity at last. But as her life is threatened repeatedly by a hidden killer, Victoria wonders if she will live long enough to find out.

**Hermes** Press

Published by Hermes Press, an imprint of
Herman and Geer Communications, Inc.

Daniel Herman, Publisher
Troy Musguire, Production Manager
Eileen Sabrina Herman, Managing Editor
Alissa Fisher, Graphic Design
Kandice Hartner, Senior Editor
Benjamin Beers, Archivist

2100 Wilmington Road
Neshannock, Pennsylvania 16105
(724) 652-0511
www.HermesPress.com; info@hermespress.com

Book design by Eileen Sabrina Herman
First printing, 2020

LCCN applied for: 10 9 8 7 6 5 4 3 2 1 0
ISBN 978-1-61345-197-7
OCR and text editing by H + G Media and Eileen Sabrina Herman
Proof reading by Eileen Sabrina Herman and Fey Wagner

From Dan, Louise, Sabrina, Jacob, Ruk'us and Noodle for D'zur and Mellow

*Acknowledgments: This book would not be possible without the help and encouragement of Jim Pierson and Curtis Holdings*

Printed in Canada

# STRANGERS AT COLLINS HOUSE
## by Marilyn Ross

# CONTENTS

# CHAPTER 1

WHEN VICTORIA WINTERS remembered that summer she would always think of the room first. For it was that room, that hidden room, which held the key to the mystery and set the scene for the many macabre events that were to follow in rapid sequence during those warm summer days and nights at Collins House.

From the rainy night so long ago when Victoria had first arrived at the bleak old mansion on Widow's Hill she had known the rambling structure with its forty rooms was a place of secrets. The tragedies of the past lay like a dark cloud over the ancient house with its slender brick chimneys straggling to the sky.

Yet it seemed there was always another mystery to be unfolded, another eerie surprise yet to be revealed. It was as if some ancient conjurer offered an illusion of boxes, one ensconced within the other, and each cunningly containing its own strange secret. During the time she had spent in the isolated Maine village of Collinsport as companion to the lovely, regal Elizabeth Collins Stoddard and as governess to young David Collins, she had come to understand many things about the old mansion and its people. Yet always there was some elusive enigma to replace the one revealed to her.

And always there was the ultimate mocking question of her own origin that had compelled her to leave her teaching position in the New York orphanage where she'd been raised and come to this remote seaport village near Bar Harbor. Time and again she had felt she was on the brink of solving this mystery so close to her and always her hopes had been dashed.

So a kind of patience had come to her. Perhaps for the first time in her life she had come to feel part of a family. Elizabeth had been good to her and Elizabeth's daughter, Carolyn, had in many ways seemed more like a younger sister than the daughter of her employer. Even the boy, David, had not been as difficult as the villagers had predicted — Victoria's kindness and understanding had worked wonders with her charge. Roger Collins, the boy's father and brother of Elizabeth, had proven unpleasant in many ways. His neglect of the family fish-packing business and his drinking constituted a scandal in Collinsport. And the fact that he was long separated from his wife and known to have a roving eye for attractive females made Victoria especially wary of him.

Yet she had found a way to live even with Roger, by giving of her best to his son and ignoring Roger's cruder remarks. To balance this unpleasant person there was his cousin, Ernest Collins, the violinist with whom she was in love. And it seemed that with the advent of summer their romance was to become an even more meaningful thing in her life. Ernest had promised to visit her between concert tours if at all possible; the tone of his letters had been ardent, and Victoria felt that with his visit might come an offer of marriage.

Not that she was certain she was ready for such an all-important venture yet. First she hoped to find out the truth about herself, and if, as she suspected, she might be related to the Collins family. Otherwise why had Elizabeth sought her out and invited her to come to Collinsport? There had to be some link between her being invited there and the monthly check sent to the orphanage for her expenses over a period of many years. The check had been mailed from Bangor, only thirty-odd miles from Collinsport. Yet Elizabeth had been stubbornly silent whenever Victoria questioned her and she had learned nothing from any of the others.

Burke Devlin, the mystery man of Collinsport, who had returned wealthy after an absence of years, had become more friendly with Victoria lately. They had enjoyed many talks together and she found him a fascinating, enigmatic man. The fact that he was a bit older and strictly devoted to his worldwide business interests, which he conducted from a suite in the Collinsport Inn, made it possible for her to enjoy his friendship without making Ernest jealous. And when she had looked to him for help one evening as they sat enjoying a late evening coffee in the lunch room of the hotel restaurant he had smiled at her across the table.

"Why not leave well enough alone, Victoria?" he asked, a hint of wistfulness on his gravely handsome face.

"You don't understand what it means to me," she'd told him. "How can I go on without ever discovering the truth about my identity?

How can I marry? Have children of my own without being able to tell them who their grandparents were?" Her lovely dark hair almost touched her shoulders, framing her thin but intelligently beautiful face.

There was a sad gleam in Burke Devlin's eyes. "Has it ever occurred to you that there are questions which are often better unanswered? Surely you know the story of Pandora's box."

"But to know who one is, that's a basic need," she insisted, looking down and toying with her half-empty coffee cup.

"It's a tormenting question, I'll admit," Burke Devlin agreed. "But life is full of such questions for many of us," he said. "Because I prefer to keep my life, business and private, strictly to myself, I'm accused of all manner of things. And I'm surely causing the wagging tongues of the town excruciating pain."

She looked up at him with a smile. "It's not a good comparison."

"All right," he said. "But remember there are other people living with unanswered questions besides yourself. I, for one. And Elizabeth for another. Don't you think she is tormented by the mystery of what happened to her husband who left her nearly twenty years ago?"

"Naturally," Victoria had agreed solemnly. "And look what it has done to her. Ruined her life! Made her a recluse! She hasn't gone outside Collins House since that night her husband disappeared. It's a wonder she hasn't gone insane!"

Burke Devlin sighed. "Elizabeth is too strong a person for that. The family and the family business would have collapsed long ago if it wasn't for her."

"I'm not as strong as Elizabeth," Victoria protested.

"I think you have much more character than you give yourself credit for," Burke Devlin said. "And one day you may prove it, even to your own satisfaction."

This conversation had taken place in June, a month before the events that centered her attention on the hidden room. But she would remember Burke's words many times and in the period of her greatest crisis they would serve to help sustain her. But at that time it was all still to happen and she had much to learn.

The letter came on a sunny afternoon in early July. Because David Collins was away for the summer at a boy's camp and Carolyn Stoddard was away working in a tourist gift shop at Bar Harbor and living there with a girl friend, Victoria found herself alone at Collins House with Elizabeth and Roger. So she met the postman on the steps of the brown old mansion and got the mail. There were a half-dozen letters and some magazines. As she turned to go in she scanned the letters quickly to see if there was one for her in Ernest's familiar hand. There was none. With a small sigh she went back inside to the shaded hallway.

Roger Collins was coming down the stairs. He usually had left for the office by this time but today he had lingered on at the house. Roger smiled sarcastically as he reached the last step and came across to greet her.

"You look disappointed," he said. "Don't tell me the mailman didn't bring you a love letter. How sad!"

She felt her cheeks crimson, but she merely said, "There are two letters for you and this magazine."

"Thank you," he said, taking them with a taunting smile. "I assume the balance of the mail is for Elizabeth." As he said this he scanned the letters she still held and then, to her complete surprise, plucked one of them out of her hand. "What's this!" he said.

It was a difficult moment for Victoria. She reached out for the letter. "It's for Mrs. Stoddard! Please give it back to me."

Roger was still studying the letter and with a careless gesture of his free hand he waved her off. "This is something you wouldn't understand," he said. "A letter from Uncle Henry! It can mean only one thing! He's planning a visit here."

"Please!" Victoria said, waiting for the letter to be returned.

He looked up at her with an unpleasant grin and still retained the letter. "Wait until you meet Uncle Henry," he said. "Now he is a real character. Outdoes all the rest of us in that regard. And of course, there's his room. His special room!" With a low, malicious laugh he finally returned the letter to her. "I'd like to see Elizabeth's face when she reads this!"

As it turned out, he didn't. He had left for the fish packing plant before Elizabeth came down and received the mail from Victoria. But Victoria was sitting with her in the big living room with its high ceiling, rich antique furniture and portraits of the Collins ancestors starting with Jeremiah, who built the house in 1830.

Elizabeth's still lovely face registered surprise and concern as she read the letter. And when she finished it she sat back in her chair with a rather strange expression.

She said, "It seems we are to have guests. And soon. They will likely be arriving sometime tomorrow."

Victoria, who had settled with a magazine on the divan across from her, said, "Relatives?"

Elizabeth nodded. "Yes, Uncle Henry Collins. He is my father's older brother and the only surviving member of all that family. Uncle Henry has always made his home in New York. He used his share of the family money for real estate in the city and I believe he is very wealthy."

"He must be quite old?" Victoria said.

"In his late seventies and not at all well."

"Then he is coming down here for his health?"

Elizabeth glanced at the letter and raised an eyebrow. "He says he is coming here to die. But then that is like Uncle Henry. He has a strong neurotic streak. It seems he suffered a serious heart attack a few months ago and has just barely recovered from it."

"Will he be well enough to make the journey?" Victoria wondered. "Has he a wife?"

"He won't be alone. He's been widowed for years but he has maintained an apartment. His employee, Benjamin Willard, has been with him so long he's more like a brother. They are both about the same age. Benjamin is also widowed and so his son and daughter-in-law have joined my uncle's household, the son as chauffeur and his wife as cook-housekeeper. They'll all make the trip here with him."

"Then he should be all right."

"They'll drive in easy stages," Elizabeth explained. "And when they arrive here they'll occupy the apartment in the rear wing that Ernest used when he lived here. We'll find another room for the son and daughter-in-law and then we'll open up Uncle Henry's special room." She paused with a weary smile. "I have no doubt that is where he'll spend most of his time unless he's changed a great deal."

Victoria was puzzled by the reference to a special room. She said, "I'm not sure I follow you."

"I'm certain you don't," Elizabeth said. "But you will very shortly. There are many sections of this big house you've never visited. We've had to keep so many rooms shut off because of lack of help and also because we have no actual need of so much space. But I can't put off showing you the hidden room any longer."

"The hidden room?"

"Yes. That is what we've always called it. It really isn't part of the regular house and has never been used by the family here. In a very special way it is Henry's room and his alone." She stood up. "But come along and I will show it to you."

Victoria was intrigued by this hint of mystery. She followed Elizabeth up the stairs to the second floor and then out the corridor to what was known as the rear wing of the house. When they arrived at the door of the apartment that Ernest had occupied, Elizabeth took a key ring from her apron pocket and unlocked the door. The hall of the apartment was dark and had a musty smell of being locked up for some time.

Elizabeth stood in the shadows. "We must clean and air it," she said. And then she moved over to what Victoria had always believed to be a closet. Looking over her shoulder, she said, "I'm sure you've never been through here."

She frowned slightly. "It's a closet, isn't it?"

The older woman smiled faintly. "A closet with a door in its rear wall. You'll see." She opened the closet door, pushed the hangers out of the way and with a second key opened this door. When she swung it open a room in almost complete darkness was revealed. "Follow me in," she ordered Victoria as she went ahead.

Victoria gingerly passed through the narrow closet to the hidden room and stood in its gloom with a sudden sense of the unusual overwhelming her. It could have been merely the darkness of this musty place after the summer sunshine that had surrounded her in the rest of the house, the eerie atmosphere of its secret entrance and gloomy shadows or, as she often felt later, it could have been something of infinitely more portent, the chilling skeleton hand of one long dead reaching out from the unknown to touch her and warn her of the danger lurking there.

"No one has been in here for several years." Elizabeth coughed as she touched the window drapes. She located the cords controlling them and suddenly drew them back. A flood of sunshine came through the dusty, cobwebbed window panes to illuminate the room.

And what a room it was!

"I've never seen anything like it before," Victoria gasped as she stared around her in a dazed fashion.

Elizabeth, her back to the window, was regarding her and smiling. "Nor are you apt to again," she said. "This room was brought here piece by piece at a great expense by Uncle Henry some forty years ago. It is a complete room with all the original furnishings taken from the famous old Ritz Hampton Hotel in New York. When the Ritz Hampton was torn down to make way for an office building Uncle Henry asked permission of my father to rebuild this room from it here. We had the space that he lacked in his New York apartment. My father agreed and so it was sent here item by item and put in place by a crew of workmen." Elizabeth raised her eyes. "Even the plaster moldings and the centerpiece of the ceiling are identical to the original room, and the light fixture is the same."

Victoria continued to stare about her, her big dark eyes wide with astonishment. "It's incredible!" she said. And it was. The room was completely different from all the rest of Collins House. It had an elegance and dignity of its own. The overwhelming impression was of crimson and ivory. The walls were in a deep crimson of richly patterned, scrolled wallpaper. The canopied bed was ivory with crimson curtains; the rich oriental rug was of yet another matching shade of red, the large mantelpiece was ivory with a huge framed print of troops assembled in orderly fashion on the slanted deck of a sinking ship; other prints of the period in rich frames of gold decorated the walls; there were easy chairs in crimson and ivory, a large rolltop desk, and several doors that must give access to closets, all decorated in the same ivory.

Elizabeth grimaced as she ran her hand over the small table. "Dust! We have a good day's work here!"

Victoria stared at her. "But what does it mean, this hidden room?

Why did your uncle salvage it and have it rebuilt this way?"

The older woman came over to her. "I told you Uncle Henry is neurotic. He is also rather sentimental." She picked up a magazine and held it for her to see. "Look at that cover. Note the date."

Victoria did so. She was touched by the quaint, old-fashioned beauty of the girl on the magazine front and she read the date aloud. "October, 1916!"

Elizabeth put the magazine down again. "Even the magazines, newspapers and calendars in here belong to the past," she said. "It is like a moment long ago preserved and when you enter here you become part of it."

She nodded solemnly as she studied the quaint room in detail. "I had a strange feeling the moment I came in here."

"So you noticed," the older woman said. "I was reasonably sure you would; you are a sensitive girl."

"But what does it mean? Why would he do such a thing? Go to such expense to satisfy a whim?"

The attractive mistress of Collins House gazed around her with a sad smile. "Because this room had a romantic meaning for him. He couldn't bear to think of its being destroyed. So much of what it stood for had been lost he couldn't stand by and allow it to fall victim to the wrecker. And so he salvaged it to enjoy for the rest of his life. To remind him of a brief interlude of love and what his life might have been. Years ago this room was the setting of a love affair between Henry Collins and a beautiful girl, now long dead. It has always been a kind of shrine for him."

Victoria was impressed. "He kept coming here all through the years!"

"And the room was kept for him exactly as you see it. Now he is returning for what may very well be a final visit. To live with his memories for a last time and perhaps die near them."

"He doesn't sound like a very happy man."

"I would hardly describe him as one," Elizabeth agreed. "Yet he does seem to find a certain contentment here. When he is at Collins House he spends more than half his time in this room."

"But is that healthy, living so much in the past?"

The older woman raised her eyebrows. "I'm afraid it is a weakness of the Collins family."

Victoria was at once embarrassed. She thought of Elizabeth's remaining in the house all these years and realized that in a sense it was a parallel to what her Uncle Henry was doing with this room.

At once she said, "I'm sorry. I shouldn't be offering comments on something which I neither understand nor am concerned about."

Elizabeth smiled generously. "Please don't apologize. This is a strange business and you were perfectly justified in expressing your opinion of it. But I know you'll like Uncle Henry. He is a charming old gentleman."

"I look forward to meeting him," Victoria said.

The older woman gave her a strange stare, holding it for just a moment. "Yes," she said, in a subdued tone. "I do believe it could have real interest for you."

At the time Victoria wasn't quite sure what Elizabeth meant. Later, however, she was to remember the moment and search for a special meaning in those apparently casual words. She said, "You think they'll arrive tomorrow?"

"That's what the letter indicated," Elizabeth said. "Of course they could be delayed. But I'm sure they'd let us know." She sighed as she studied the carpet. "The whole room needs doing and quickly. Ask Matt Morgan to come in and vacuum the rug and drapes. I know he'll complain and say he's only supposed to do outside work."

"Perhaps I could do it," Victoria suggested. She knew what a fuss Matt would raise.

Elizabeth shook her head. "I won't give way to him in this. We'll have plenty of other cleaning to take care of. To make things worse, Matt and Benjamin, Uncle Henry's companion, seem to have a natural antipathy for each other. They quarreled whenever their paths crossed the last summer Uncle Henry came here."

"Perhaps it will be different this time."

"I doubt it. Benjamin is a nice old man, but quick-tempered and dour. I'd be afraid that he'd be worse now that he's a few years older."

Victoria smiled. "They say age mellows."

"I think it applies only to whiskey," the older woman said as she moved slowly about the room taking stock of what was to be done. "I doubt if he will be doing much. His son and daughter-in-law take over most of the work now. Benjamin serves chiefly as companion to Unde Henry."

"What are the son and daughter like?"

Elizabeth frowned. "Not memorable, that's certain. I seem to think of them as rather ordinary in type. The son is loud and bossy, middle-aged, the race track type, and as I recall, his wife was thin, whiny and no beauty."

"They don't sound too prepossessing."

"They're not. We can be thankful we haven't any other servants besides Matt to get involved with them. We'd probably be in hot water all the time. And then there is Roger. He dislikes Uncle Henry almost as much as Uncle Henry hates him."

"I hadn't any idea," she said, although she did recall Roger's brazen behavior with the letter.

"Just another problem to cope with," Elizabeth said with an attempt to be cheerful. "I'll open a window before we leave and let some fresh air in here."

When Roger came home for dinner there was nearly a scene at the long table in the big dining room. "I suppose Uncle Henry is really coming," he said, as a beginning.

"Yes, tomorrow," Elizabeth said.

"Imposition!" Roger said with annoyance. "I'm sick of catering to that old man." He gave Victoria a sinister glance. "I suppose you've been introduced to the hidden room!"

"She has done better than that," Elizabeth said, picking the question up for her. "She helped clean it up."

"I can't imagine why father ever consented to its being brought here in the first place," Roger grumbled over his plate. And with a meaningful glance for his sister, "Especially when you consider the dark history connected with it."

"It's not a subject I care to discuss," Elizabeth said coldly. "And I'm sure that Victoria isn't interested."

Roger's smile was malicious. "It's all right with me," he said. "We'll omit any references to Uncle Henry and his friends if that's what you want."

"I think it would be wise," his sister said. To Victoria, she added, "When you write to Ernest, let him know we've heard from Uncle Henry. He always took a great interest in the old man."

Roger said, "Let Ernest tell you about Uncle Henry. You are bound to find it fascinating."

Again Elizabeth changed the subject and Victoria was aware of the tension between her and her brother. She was sure that she hadn't heard all the story connected with this room transplanted so completely from its original site, yet she couldn't imagine what it might be. Because of the way Roger gloated over his sister's uneasiness when the subject was brought up Victoria suspected that it might not be pleasant, that behind the apparent eccentricity of Uncle Henry there might be shadow of tragedy.

This thought pursued her all through the night and day before the arrival of the old man and his entourage. No subsequent word had been received from him, so Elizabeth was expecting they would come in the late afternoon in time for dinner.

Victoria was given the task of finishing up the apartment and the hidden room, checking to see that clean linen was available in sufficient quantity and that all the other last minute touches were in order. It was close to four when she completed the job.

Leaving the apartment, she went through the short corridor that had been so successfully camouflaged as a closet and entered the crimson and white hidden room. For no reason that she understood it had a true fascination for her. And now as she stood in the center of the elegant old room, lost in the atmosphere of another age, she tried to puzzle why it should exert such an influence on her.

Perhaps because it was so different. Certainly not because of any sense of ease or contentment it brought her, for she felt far from relaxed within its walls. The room induced a definite tension in her, a feeling that it had been the setting of some scene of violence which she did not know about, a brooding calm that had followed after some fearful eruption in the past.

Staring about her at the faded elegance of it all, she was filled with a definite nostalgia, a sense of the quick passing of time and the changes it wrought. She let her eyes wander from the rich red velvet drapes at the high window to the white marble fireplace taller than she was and to the gold-framed print above it. What had happened to the girl whom Uncle Henry had loved, she wondered? How had the two met and what had finally parted them? Was the entire story of the romance linked with this single room? And had the dark doings about which Roger had so pointedly hinted any bearing on it all?

Standing there in the silence, the beauty of the room enriched by the late afternoon sun that still imparted slim rays of gold to mingle with the shadows of another age, she pondered on all these things. She was wearing a white afternoon dress, plain and simply styled, that seemed to go well with the surroundings. And the white bow with which she'd temporarily knotted her long dark hair while working gave her the quaint look of the girl whose lovely face stared at her from the cover of the magazine on the table near her.

She moved slowly across to the table and picked up a yellowed newspaper that lay next to the magazine. Opening it she read its date and saw that it was October 31, 1916. A half-century had passed since it had brought its report of a day's happenings.

Putting the paper down again, she was suddenly aware of the significance of the date. October 31 was Halloween! The night of witches and goblins when the darkness came early and the evil spirits played their pranks!

So time had stopped in this old room on a long ago Hallows Eve! Why? What had happened on that night of mystery to make it so significant? She stared at the ancient newspaper with troubled eyes.

And then she heard a soft sound from behind her. It came as a surprise and she turned quickly to see a frail, slightly-stooped figure standing in the doorway of the room.

His hair was silver white, his face sallow and patrician, and he was dressed in sober black. But his eyes were too bright for the weary old body, and were fixed on her now with sheer amazement. She saw the old man's lips move as if forming words but nothing issued from them. And inexplicably a cold chill tightened around her heart.

# CHAPTER 2

A ND THEN THE old man spoke and the strange spell was broken. "You must be Victoria," he said in a mellow, pleasant voice as he came slowly into the room, his eyes still studying her.

She managed a smile. "And you must be Mr. Henry Collins."

He extended a thin hand. "That is correct. We arrived a little early and I couldn't wait to get up here. Finding you in the room gave me a start."

"I'm sorry. I was finishing the cleaning. I intended to be done before you got here."

"Don't apologize," he said with a sad smile on his lined, aristocratic face. "I am glad to have discovered you in this setting." He paused. "Believe me when I say you are very right for this room."

His eyes were still intent upon her; she was not sure she knew what he was trying to convey. She glanced about her. "It is a fascinating room. I didn't even know about it until a few days ago."

He nodded. "It is my special interest. I'm glad you approve. It seems fitting that you should." Again there was an insinuation in his words that left her puzzled.

"What a unique idea," she said. "To restore a room this way. It's like a kind of museum."

Henry Collins smiled another of his sad smiles. "I can imagine it must seem that to you. But for me it is something quite different. A reminder of a fine hotel, a gracious fragment of an age much more fulfilling than the one we know now, the last of the really golden eras."

Victoria returned his smile. "Yet you must have been fairly young when the Ritz Hampton was at its peak of popularity."

"True," he acknowledged. "And even then things were starting to change. The New York that had been four or five stories high was beginning to reach for the clouds. The shopping district had moved from Twenty-Third Street up the hill and along two miles of Fifth Avenue. We had the telephone, the electric light, the trolley car, typewriter, gramophones, motion pictures, airplanes and automobiles, with business offices full of bright young girls like yourself."

She shook her head. "You amaze me. I have been picturing an earlier period with horse-drawn cars and hansom cabs, women in long skirts and flowing veils."

The old man laughed softly. "There were plenty of long skirts and flowing veils, and large magnificent hats such as we don't see women wearing anymore. We even had our share of hansom cabs and horse-driven vehicles until much later. So your imaginings are not so wrong."

"Perhaps it was a transition period," she suggested, "a linking of the old and the new."

"In a very real sense. And then the war came to change everything. When it ended we were in a totally different period that led to the Second World War and this automated, sterile world we live in today."

"You don't sound too enthusiastic about it."

"In spite of lovely young people like yourself, I'm not," he admitted with a sigh. "And don't think we were so old-fashioned. These frugs and other discotheque dances of your day aren't a bit more daring than were our turkey-trots, or a waist bending exercise named the maxixe and a queer, zoological antic named the lame duck."

"It sounds fascinating and very advanced," Victoria laughed.

"I promise you we considered ourselves very modern," he said. Again he looked piercingly at Victoria. "Have you come to like this strange old house?"

"In a way it has come to mean home for me," she said, serious again. "The only one I have ever really known."

"I'm glad to hear you say that," Henry Collins said. "For some young girls it might be an ordeal to live here so remote from the town, in an ancient building filled with ghosts of the past."

"I think the past can be very exciting. I was always thrilled by my history studies."

He eyed her approvingly. "Yes. I can see you might really appreciate such things. We must talk some more about those other days."

They were interrupted by the appearance of another elderly man carrying a suitcase. Victoria guessed him to be Benjamin Willard, Henry's companion. He appeared the same age as Henry Collins, but he was a larger man with a gaunt face, deep-set eyes and a completely bald head. He wore a dark gray suit.

Henry at once confirmed her guess by introducing her to the newcomer. "Victoria Winters, Mr. Benjamin Willard, who sees that I take some sort of care of myself," he said genially. "You've already heard about Miss Winters, Benjamin."

The taller old man shook hands with her. "Yes. It is a pleasure to meet you, Miss Winters," he said in a gruff voice. And he gave her such a thorough stare that she at once felt self-conscious again.

"You're familiar with the apartment," she said.

"Indeed," Benjamin Willard assured her. And to Henry, he said, "I assume we will be taking the usual rooms."

"Yes," Henry Collins told him. "Elizabeth is providing rooms on this floor for your son and daughter-in-law, but in the main wing."

"Very good," Benjamin said rather stiffly. "I'll take this bag to your room then." And with a nod to Victoria, he said, "Nice meeting you, Miss Winters." With that he left them.

Henry Collins regarded her with an amused glance. "When someone has lived with you as long as Benjamin has lived with me he ceases to be a servant and becomes an old friend."

"I'm sure you must feel that way," she said.

"Benjamin is one of the main solaces of my declining years," he confessed. "One of the few who really understands and remembers the things that I remember. Such as this room."

Victoria smiled. "I hope you are feeling better and have a nice vacation here."

"I'm as well as I can expect to be," the old man said. And with an old-fashioned gallantry he added, "Finding you here assures me of an enjoyable visit."

She left him standing there in the hidden room alone. He seemed anxious to remain there awhile. Victoria was filled with mixed feelings about the old man. He had seemed friendly; yet there was an air of mystery and sadness about him that matched the atmosphere of the room itself. And she was puzzled by the way he had stared at her and his references to her belonging in the room. Had there been a secret meaning in his words and if so, what was it?

As she reached the juncture of the main corridor of the old house she met a stout, middle-aged man in a chauffeur's uniform, laden with suitcases. She knew by his facial resemblance to Benjamin

Willard that he must be his son.

Smiling at the man, she said, "Mr. Collins and Mr. Willard are already in the apartment."

"Thanks!" The stout man said rather breathlessly and pushed on with the bags. Elizabeth's description of him had been accurate. He looked like a drinker and the race track type.

In the corridor of the main house Elizabeth was in the act of showing a thin woman of about her own age into a room. She paused to smile and tell Victoria, "Mrs. Molly Willard, this is Miss Victoria Winters."

Molly Willard had a worn, sullen face that had once been pretty. She was dressed shabbily and her straw-colored hair was wispy and dyed-looking. Her pale blue eyes took Victoria in with dull interest and in a reedy voice she said, "Pleased to meetcha!"

Victoria nodded. "I went over the kitchen. I think you'll find everything you need. And Mrs. Stoddard has ordered a general stock of provisions."

Elizabeth added, "I think there is a good supply, but you can phone the village if there should be extras you want and they'll deliver in the morning."

Molly Willard picked up her suitcase. "Yes, Mrs. Stoddard," she said in the same unpleasant voice and went into the room assigned to her.

Elizabeth turned to Victoria with a relieved look on her attractive face and said as they strolled toward the stairs, "Well, I think we have everyone settled."

"Your Uncle Henry is a very interesting man," Victoria told her.

"I think so," her employer agreed. "I'm glad to see him looking as well as he does. But then, in heart cases you never can tell. Certainly he is happy to be back here."

"He came to the room at once," Victoria said. "And he was still there when I left him."

Elizabeth paused at the head of the stairs a moment to show her interest. "You were in the hidden room when he arrived. Did he seem startled to find you there?"

Victoria smiled. "He did act a little strange. He stared at me in a most peculiar way."

"Put it down to his not expecting to have a pretty girl waiting for him there," she said. "I expect he'll think I arranged it especially for his benefit."

Victoria glanced at her in surprise. "Why would he think that?"

Elizabeth seemed embarrassed. "I can't imagine," she said quickly. "I don't know why I expressed myself in those particular words." They had come to the lower hall and there were several large black cases there. Seeing that Victoria had noticed them, the older woman told her, "Those belong to Benjamin. He makes a hobby of astronomy. Those cases contain his telescope and other equipment. I expect he'll be setting them up on the roof somewhere. He always has before."

Victoria took another look at the cases. "They seem heavy."

"They are," Elizabeth assured her. "He'll get his son, Jack, to take them up in due time. I imagine you met him. He's wearing a chauffeur's uniform."

"We met in the corridor. He looks a good deal like his father."

Elizabeth nodded. "Yes. But the similarity ends with that. Old Benjamin is a true gentleman, while Jack and his wife are rough characters. I've heard that they've cost the old man a lot. Jack is shiftless and if it wasn't for this work provided them by Uncle Henry I can't imagine how they would exist."

"Will Mr. Collins be having dinner with us tonight?" Victoria asked.

The older woman nodded. "I give him a standing invitation to dine with us whenever he likes. Often he has his meals at the apartment, chiefly because of his health, but I think too that he enjoys his privacy. But he invariably takes his place at the table with us on the first night of his arrival."

"He has so many interesting things to talk about," Victoria said. "Just now he was telling me about old New York, and the changes that have taken place in the city over the years."

Elizabeth looked thoughtful. "Yes, he would surely be able to tell you about that. You'll have a chance to know him better at dinner. Uncle Henry has always been a good conversationalist."

Victoria privately wondered how it would be with Roger and the old man at the table together. Since Roger had complained so bitterly about his coming on the previous day, she hoped he wouldn't make it unpleasant for the old gentlemen. Henry Collins deserved better treatment. But in her rush to help Elizabeth with dinner she didn't have too much time to worry about the problem. When they had finished preparing the dessert, an old-fashioned strawberry shortcake, the older woman insisted she go upstairs and get ready for dinner.

"You must look your best for Uncle Henry's sake," Elizabeth said with a smile. "I want him to enjoy himself. And I'd like you to make a good impression on him."

Victoria didn't argue, but again she felt that Elizabeth was secretly excited about something. And she wondered why she was so determined to have her impress the old man so favorably. Perhaps Elizabeth hoped to offset the bad behavior she feared from Roger.

Taking a quick shower, she changed into a cool, shadowy voile. She had removed the bow from her hair and now took some time combing it out and arranging it to her satisfaction. When she made her appearance downstairs Roger was standing in the doorway of the living room, holding a cocktail glass.

He gave her an appreciative glance and took a sip from the glass. "My, we look mighty attractive tonight," he said. "So sister dear has you on exhibition!"

Victoria frowned slightly and felt her cheeks warm. "I'm afraid I don't follow you."

Roger smiled wryly. "Maybe you don't, but I can promise you Elizabeth knows what she is up to. You're the special treat to make the evening for our respected Uncle Henry!"

"I hardly think that," she protested.

"You look luscious," Roger insisted, annoyingly. "And I have no doubt you'll be a ravishing success."

Elizabeth came down the stairs, wearing a chic white gown that brought out her dark beauty. There seemed no doubt she had overheard part of their talk, for her attractive face was shadowed. Going straight over to Roger, she faced him defiantly. "I hope you're not drinking too much," she said. "I'd like to feel I could count on you to conduct yourself properly for once."

He spread a hand innocently and insisted, "I'm just having a single cocktail to put me in the mood for Uncle Henry. I thought I might entertain him with a cozy discussion of the Harry K. Thaw murder case."

It meant nothing to Victoria but seemed to incense Elizabeth. Her lovely eyes flashed fire. "How dare you even think about such a thing!"

"Why not?" Roger went on in his bantering fashion. "I happen to know Uncle was a friend of the victim, Sanford White, and without a doubt he'd have been an admirer of Evelyn Nesbit!" He glanced at Victoria. "Have you ever heard of the 'Girl In The Red Velvet Swing'?"

Elizabeth turned to her with a warning look. "Don't pay any attention to him, Victoria. It's his poor idea of humor!"

Roger sipped his cocktail again and chuckled. "Or I could rave     about the beauty of the Gibson girls! Come to think of it, Victoria resembles a Gibson-girl!"

Again the reference was lost on Victoria. Elizabeth seemed to understand him and while his comment didn't actually make her angry this time, she looked tense and unhappy. "Would it hurt you to show a little kindness for once?" she asked her brother.

He bowed. "Count on me. I'll be the perfect host. After all, it is sort of fitting that Uncle Henry should come back here. A man of mystery returns to the house of mystery." Roger might have gone on tormenting his sister with his black humor if the old man hadn't suddenly appeared on the stairs. He wore a dinner jacket with black tie and made his way down slowly, using the bannister and a silver-headed cane for support.

True to his usual hypocrisy, Roger hurried across to meet him and shake his hand as if it gave him great pleasure. Henry accepted the attention with what Victoria thought was ironic amusement and allowed his nephew to fetch him a drink.

When they were all standing in the living room in a group Roger said, "I've just been paying Victoria the ultimate in compliments, Uncle. I've told her she looks like a Gibson girl. Don't you agree?"

Henry smiled at her. "You do have a hint of her. Roger is very perceptive." He raised his glass. "A toast to Victoria, our Gibson girl. May she always be with us."

Feeling the center of attention and not knowing why, Victoria sipped the wine Elizabeth had given her and realized she was blushing furiously. Elizabeth gave her an encouraging glance and seemed to be cynically entertained by her brother's performance.

Now Henry turned to Victoria affably. "Perhaps I should explain what we mean by the Gibson girl—although a few years ago that would have been thought ridiculously unnecessary. She was the creation of a noted artist, Charles Dana Gibson. Not far from here, in Bar Harbor as a matter of record, he met and fell in love with a southern beauty, Irene Langhorne, who was to become his wife and the model for his drawings of lovely young women from that time on. He drew sketches of many beauties, but those of his wife became the best known."

"Thank you for the explanation and the compliment," Victoria said with a special smile for the old gentleman.

"Bravo!" Roger said too loudly, obviously sneering at them all. "Victoria, you have a neat turn with a phrase that I never suspected."

Elizabeth spoke up. "It's time we went in to dinner."

They made an interesting company around the table in the lovely old dining room. Elizabeth had the various dishes ready on the sideboard, a necessity with no maid available. For a time the conversation lagged in deference to the excellent cold salmon, little peas, garden-fresh, and new potatoes. Not until they had finished with the strawberry dessert and began to relax over coffee and liqueurs did the talk become spirited again.

"The drive down here was magnificent," Henry Collins said. "And I was struck by the number of changes in the village. There is a fine new home just being built on the outskirts. Have you seen it,

Elizabeth?"

There was a pause. Then from the head of the table Elizabeth answered quietly, "No. I'm afraid I haven't."

The old man raised his eyebrows in mild surprise. "Really, I can't think how you could have missed it!" Then he flushed, as if suddenly remembering that she hadn't left Collins House for almost twenty years. "I'm sorry. Blame it on an old man's feeble memory. I'd completely forgotten you never go to the village."

"Elizabeth never goes anywhere!" Roger said with a smile that was meant to annoy. "But then, we don't think about it any more."

Victoria, wanting to help the situation, told the old man quickly, "The talk in town is that it is being built for a millionaire who has returned here lately. A Mr. Burke Devlin. Perhaps you know him?"

Henry shook his head. "I can't say that I do."

Roger looked sullen at the mention of Burke Devlin, as he always did. "I doubt very much if that story is true," he said. "I can't see Devlin staying in Collinsport long."

Elizabeth gave her brother an innocent glance. "I had no idea you and Burke had become such close friends that you would know what he had in mind."

Victoria waited with some tension to see how Roger would react; if Elizabeth's words would trigger him to worse behavior.

Roger scowled. "I hear a few things around the village, as well." And then with a change of mood he turned to the old man, "It is too bad you didn't arrive in time for the Fourth of July celebration here," he observed.

"Really?" Henry Collins seemed vaguely puzzled.

"Oh, yes," Roger assured him. "Collinsport does famously by Independence day. It has a certain flavor here. Have you ever noticed how special days seem to suit various localities? Consider Christmas and you think of London." He paused and glanced Elizabeth's way. "And when I think of Halloween I always link it with New York. A dark autumn evening, crisp and cool, in old New York. Doesn't that strike you as odd?"

Victoria couldn't help looking at Henry, knowing this remark must have been directed to him for a purpose. There had been no mistaking the triumphantly ugly expression on Roger's face when he'd turned to Elizabeth before speaking. And now she saw that the old man's face had paled and the hand that held the liqueur glass trembled slightly.

"I haven't given it any thought," he said in a dry voice. Roger was all smiles now, thoroughly enjoying himself. "Hallow's Eve, a time of pagan festival. Goes back to the Druids, they say. The masks and costumes all part of it. Those grotesque false faces always make me think of the twisted, ugly souls of those who wear them. I have a theory that people select masks that betray them for the characters they really are!"

Remembering the date of the ancient paper in the hidden room, Victoria knew October 31 must have a special meaning for Henry Collins, perhaps a tragic meaning, and Roger was tormenting him about it. Victoria tried to ease the tension by admonishing Roger, "Surely you must be wrong. Most of the dressing-up and costuming at Halloween is done by youngsters."

"Doesn't change my views at all," Roger assured her with a twisted smile. "In some uncanny way they look ahead and prophesy what they are going to become. The gnarled mask of the miser is a glance at things to come for the lad who wears it and was attracted to it intuitively in the first place. The wanton mask of a temptress on some lovely little girl is a penetrating glimpse into her future."

Elizabeth spoke up from the head of the table. "I don't remember clearly, but in that case I would suspect you must have selected a mask of Satan when you were a youngster."

He nodded mockingly. "Your score, dear sister." And addressing himself to the old man again who was finishing the last of his liqueur, Roger went on, "I think of Halloween as a time of mad carnival, when the evil in man has a chance to revel in the dark autumn night. And what better spot to focus on man's evil and murderous nature than the carnal canyons of Manhattan!"

There was the sharp sound of splintering glass as Henry Collins let the liqueur glass slip. The old man stared down in consternation and then turned to Elizabeth, his face deathly white. "I am sorry," he said. "How clumsy of me!"

"Don't think about it, Uncle Henry," Elizabeth said at once. "Would you care for another liqueur?"

"Thank you, no!" the old man said hastily and leaning heavily on his cane, he raised himself from his chair. "I am not feeling quite myself. If you will be so kind as to excuse me I will go upstairs."

"Let me go with you," Elizabeth said as they all rose from the table. She went over to touch a solicitous hand to the old man's arm.

He shook his head. "It's not necessary, I assure you. I'm just a little weary and I would prefer to go alone." And with a bow that included them all he moved across the room and made his exit with dignity.

Elizabeth waited until he had gone and then she looked directly at her brother. "I hope you're satisfied," she said.

Roger dropped his napkin by his plate and moved away from the table with a sheepish expression. "I was only trying to make small talk," he said.

Elizabeth sighed. "I know very well what you were trying to

do and so do you."

Roger gave another of his nasty smiles. "My conscience is completely clear. I must say I don't understand you at all." And with that he left the dining room.

Victoria stood there with the older woman alone for several long minutes of silence. She knew that somehow Roger had badly upset the old man and left his sister almost equally disturbed. But since this was a family thing, she felt she could not show her curiosity—even though she was frustrated by being on the perimeter of their talk.

Elizabeth broke the silence with a deep sigh. "We may as well begin to clear up," she said.

All during the clearing up in the dining room and later in the kitchen when they were washing the dishes, Victoria thought the older woman might break her silence and explain what the conversation at the table had been all about. And why Roger's remarks had produced such a violent reaction in old Henry Collins. But Elizabeth had decided to be tight-lipped on the subject and said not a word. When they finished she excused herself, saying she had a headache, and went upstairs also.

Left alone, Victoria planned to take a walk along the cliff. It was a lovely summer evening and she had found in the past the solitude and bracing air often helped clear her mind and let her see things in a different light. As she made her way along the winding path she turned and looked back along the coast. From here she could see Ernest's house, now rented to summer people, and she felt a deep loneliness surge through her. If only Ernest would come back it would all be different. She could frankly ask him about the mystery surrounding Henry Collins and be sure of getting an explanation.

Ernest had meant so much to her that she missed him greatly. His last letter had hinted of a short visit in Collinsport, but she dare not let herself hope too much. If he didn't come, the letdown would be painful. Now she approached the high point of the cliffs where the drop to the rocky beach below was almost a hundred feet. There was a bench there and she sat down for a moment, lost in her own thoughts and listening to the regular wash of the waves.

So intent was she that she did not hear the approaching footsteps until the stranger was coming close to her. With a startled expression she looked up and saw the chauffeur, Jack Willard, standing there. He was dressed in gray slacks and a loudly-patterned sports jacket of a lighter shade with his shirt open at the neck. He looked entirely different from when he was in uniform and somehow more bloated and disreputable.

With a smile on his coarse face he said, "Well, we meet again!"

She nodded. "Yes. Isn't it nice out here?"

He gave her a wise smile and sat down beside her. "The company is nice anyway." She was at once on her guard. Some intuitive voice told her that any encouragement given Jack Willard could produce trouble. He asked, "What do you do in this place for excitement, girlie?"

"Not much, I'm afraid," she said. "There is a movie in town and a lounge and bar called the Blue Whale. You and your wife might enjoy going there." She made the reference to his wife pointed so he would understand.

He looked disgusted. "Don't worry about my wife. I'm the one that's hard to please. This place is a dump. A regular dump! Why couldn't old Henry have picked somewhere in Maine near Portland? Then I could have had some action at the races."

"Portland is quite a drive from here," she said.

"Don't I know it," he complained. "I'd never make it up and back in an evening. And my father expects me to always be around in case the old man has a bad spell and has to be rushed to a doctor."

Victoria asked, "Is he really that ill?"

"You can't tell about him." Jack Willard's swarthy face showed annoyance. "He almost croaked a little while ago, but some of those fancy doctors got him through it."

"Maybe he'll rest down here."

"I know why he comes down here and it ain't for rest," the chauffeur said darkly. "You seen that nutty room of his?"

She nodded. "Yes."

"He sits in there most of the time. Enough to give you the creeps. My old man's just as bad. A couple of crazies! He's gone on this astronomy thing." He looked in the direction of Collins House. "He's up on your roof right now setting up his stuff."

Victoria followed his glance and saw the tiny figure on the distant roof. Benjamin Willard was setting up his telescope on the captain's walk. And it should certainly be a vantage point from which to do his stargazing.

She said, "He should be able to see plenty of stars up there."

Jack Willard swung around and with a quick movement let his arm drop down to encircle her. "I'd be satisfied with just the stars in your eyes, girlie," he said with a grin.

She quickly got up. "Let's understand one another from the start," she said. "I'm not interested in your kind of astronomy!"

Jack Willard was on his feet now and tightening his belt in a nervous gesture of indignation. "So you're one of those dames!" he said with disgust. "The way I hear it, you're just a servant here like the rest of us. Why try and play it important?"

"I promise to keep my place, Mr. Willard," she said. "Just you remember to keep yours. And you also might keep in mind you're a married man!"

"Let me worry about that!" he snapped.

"I imagine it worries your poor wife a lot more." She turned and started back to the house, leaving him standing there in a rage. It was another unhappy complication about which she'd been apprehensive ever since they had arrived. A glance at the timorous Molly Willard had shown her that the faded blonde had little or no spirit left and her husband was every inch a coarse, leering male. It spelled trouble unless the lines were clearly drawn. She hoped she had made them clear enough for Jack Willard!

As she started upstairs she decided it might be a good idea to stop by the apartment and see if Henry Collins had everything he needed. So instead of going to her own room she took the corridor to the rear wing and apartment. Even though it was only early evening the corridor was already shadowed. The apartment door was open and there was a strange silence over everything that made her feel a slight concern. Suppose Henry Collins had taken a seizure while Benjamin was on the roof?

Tentatively she entered the open door of the apartment and looked in its small living room. No one was in sight. Then she had an idea and took the route through the closet to the hidden room, whose door also happened to be ajar. The old man was not in there either.

Soft evening light made the room look different and all at once she was aware of a perfume in the air. A light fragrance, as if the lovely creature who wore it had a moment ago passed through the room. She stood there with a puzzled expression on her pretty face. Could it have been Elizabeth? But Elizabeth never wore this special perfume!

And then her attention was taken by a calendar, a small one, that had been left on one of the easy chairs. She went over and picked it up from the seat of the chair and studied it. The calendar was for the year 1916 and she was looking at the month of October. Ringed with a pencil marking was October 31, Halloween!

# CHAPTER 3

THERE COULD BE no doubt that this date had a significant meaning for Henry Collins and was related in some way to the room in which she stood. Even the calendar which she held in her hand bore an engraving in color of the long forgotten Ritz Hampton Hotel. She stared at the circled date and wondered.

Roger Collins knew the secret. She was certain of that. It explained the way he had none-too-subtly brought Halloween and New York City into the talk at the dinner table and the odd manner in which his uncle had reacted to it. She had feared for a moment the old man might have an attack then and there! But why had he become so badly upset at Roger's words?

Still studying the small calendar, she lifted the leaf showing October and looked at November. Again she was presented by an enigma. For beside every day of the month in November was a neat tiny question mark. They extended through the entire month. Her curiosity further whetted, she turned to December and to her surprise the question marks continued until December 18. This date was circled by a pencil in exactly the same fashion as October 31. There were no more of the neatly penciled question marks.

It offered a fascinating puzzle. She could only surmise the two dates were definitely connected in some way, that Henry Collins had been in doubt about something that was at last resolved on

December 18. But what had he been in doubt about and how was it resolved? The calendar provided no answers to those tantalizing questions, although it presented the skeleton outline of what had taken place.

"Where did you find that?" It was Henry Collins speaking sharply from behind her.

She wheeled about quickly and with some embarrassment said, "On the chair seat. I hope you don't mind my having looked at it."

The old man's aged, handsome face showed anger and he snatched the calendar from her. "What right have you to interfere with my private possessions?" he demanded.

Victoria was dismayed that her mission should be so misconstrued. She said, "I'm sorry. I didn't know it had any importance."

The bright eyes burned into her. "Every item in this room is of vital importance to me. Why did you come here?"

"To see if you needed anything. I thought I'd check before I went up to my own room."

"If I require anything I shall certainly ask for it. There was no need for you to intrude."

She lowered her eyes. "Again, I'm sorry," she said quietly. "I meant well. I looked at the calendar merely to fill in the time while I was waiting for you to appear."

"I'm not interested in your motives. Just don't do it again!"

"You may be certain that I won't," she said and started for the door.

"One moment!" he called after her.

She turned, puzzled by his anger and strangeness. Looking at him with a direct, challenging gaze, she said, "Yes?"

The old man stood there in the middle of the crimson and ivory room, a fitting figure for his surroundings, much more of that long ago world than the one which he had lingered to endure now. He held up the calendar. "You've studied this," he said. "Have you any idea what it means? Why I have kept it all these years?"

She shook her head. "No."

He regarded her grimly, as if not convinced she was being truthful. Then he said, "In that case I'll say nothing more. And don't come here again unless you are invited."

"I'll remember," she assured him and she left with his angry words of reprimand still echoing in her mind. It was painfully humiliating to be treated like a bad child, when she had merely hoped to be of some service to him.

Perhaps it was to be expected in someone old and ailing like himself. And he was neurotic where the hidden room was concerned.

She was more than ever certain that he remembered it not because of a long lost romance but because of some tragic incident that must have happened there. Something to do with Halloween!

It wasn't until she was in her own room that she thought about the scent of perfume that had greeted her when she'd first gone into the crimson and ivory refuge. What had it meant? Who had been in that room just before her? The exquisite fragrance had a delicate quality that made her think more of the lost age of elegance represented by the room than of the present. And then a strange thought crossed her mind. Could a ghost wear perfume?

Had some spirit graced the shadowed silence of the old hotel room just before she'd entered? Some lovely specter from the past drawn to the room by the presence of Henry Collins? Perhaps the long-dead beauty who had visited there in those long ago happier days? Was that why the old man had brought out the calendar and was that his reason for being so angry with her? Had he resented her intrusion in the room when he'd been expecting to entertain the ghost of his lost love?

It was too ridiculous. Yet, she had smelled that perfume! She could recall it vividly even now, some little time afterward. What new mystery had Henry Collins brought with him to the rambling mansion by the sea? And what was the tragedy that had transformed him from a normal human being to someone who dedicated his life to a sealed room from the past?

Burke Devlin had warned her of the danger of opening closed doors, of the hazards in asking questions that might better not be asked and risking the weight of answers that might crush her into unhappiness. Perhaps she had warranted the old man's heated words. Without realizing it, she may have been prompted by an underlying curiosity to go to that room tonight.

Upset by what had happened, for she had deep sympathy for the feeble old man, she went to bed early. The arrival of Henry Collins faced her with many new problems—among them, the aggressive, skirt-chasing Jack Willard. The beefy chauffeur's brazen advances had been the first unpleasant shock of the evening. She saw in him a greater source of annoyance than Roger Collins had ever offered. From the time she'd let Roger know she didn't appreciate any romantic interest he might have in her he'd let her strictly alone. She hoped her sharp reproval of the chauffeur would bring the same results... But she couldn't be sure!

The weather had been good most of the summer thus far and the next day was no exception. The sun was bright and there was hardly a breeze stirring. When she went down to breakfast Elizabeth remarked on her looking peaked.

"You've been working hard these last few days," the older woman said. "I want you to take it easier today. Why don't you go for a swim this morning?"

Victoria demurred. "I can think about swimming after I help you."

"There's very little to do," Elizabeth insisted. "And Uncle Henry has his own staff to look after him. So that needn't concern us." She paused. "I doubt if we'll see much of him from now on. At least in the main part of the house."

"You mean he stays up there alone all the time?"

"Most of it. Except for the company of Benjamin, he's entirely by himself. They occasionally take a stroll on the grounds. But I doubt if Henry will join us for a meal again until he is ready to leave. And perhaps not then, after the awful way Roger behaved last night."

Victoria was embarrassed by the reference to the way Roger had acted. She had tried to pretend she hadn't noticed. Now she said, "He seems to resent the old man and enjoy teasing him."

"Roger has always had a strong streak of cruelty," the other woman said. "He deliberately baited Henry last night."

"I made a bad error myself," Victoria confessed. "I stopped by the apartment before I went up to bed, just to see if he had everything he needed. I couldn't find him. While I was waiting in the hidden room he came in. He seemed terribly upset at my being there."

Elizabeth looked at her with understanding. "I'm sure he didn't mean it. He is old and apt to behave erratically at times. He'll likely forget all about it."

Victoria continued, "The odd thing is that he seemed delighted when he first arrived and found me in the room yesterday. He even said I had a right to be there!"

Elizabeth's lovely eyes widened. "He said that!"

"Yes. I didn't quite understand. I guess he meant my dress sort of suggested those old days. And I had a bow in my hair at the time."

"Of course," the older woman said quickly. "I'm sure that must have been what made him say that." But there was something in the way she rushed over the subject that made Victoria wonder.

She worked in the kitchen with Elizabeth for a while longer and then went upstairs to change into her bathing suit. Carolyn had given her a blue and white one that she had tired of and it happened to fit her very well. She put it on now, collected a large towel and a smaller one, a container of suntan lotion and a paperback novel, and hurried back down again to get to the beach.

Pausing on the front steps, she slipped her sunglasses on.

As she did so she saw Henry Collins and Benjamin Willard coming around the side of the house from the rear garden. They were walking slowly, Benjamin lending an arm to his employer who was using his silver-headed cane as always. Apparently Henry recognized her, for he paused and raised his hand in a wave of greeting.

Victoria returned the wave and then quickly crossed the lawn to the path leading down to the rather narrow beach. The tide was out, giving her more beach area than usual. After spreading out the towel she applied a good covering of lotion on her already bronzed skin until her shapely body was shining. Then she stretched out on the towel to luxuriate in the sun and read for awhile.

Time passed quickly. When she wearied of reading she watched a tiny boat drift slowly across the horizon. She wished that Carolyn was there with her for company, but since she was working and living in Bar Harbor she used the beach there. Elizabeth's daughter had no need to work and this job in a summer gift shop was chiefly a lark, a chance to be away from the somber atmosphere of Collins House for a while.

Now Victoria decided it was time to take a swim. She approached the ocean water cautiously and after the first chill of the salt water waited for a few minutes. When she finally dived in she rapidly got over the shock of it and began to enjoy the water. Because she was alone at an isolated section of beach, she did not venture out too far or remain in the ocean very long. She waded back to shore, panting from her exertions, but feeling much better.

Slipping off her bathing cap, she fluffed her long black hair and taking the smaller of the towels began drying herself. She had no more than completed this when she heard someone coming down the path. With a questioning look she turned and saw to her surprise that it was none other than Benjamin Willard.

Benjamin advanced solemnly across the sand to come and stand by her. "I saw you swimming just now," he said, with a smile on his gaunt face. "You did very well."

Victoria stood up, her towel still in hand. "I'm not very good," she apologized. "And I'm a little timid when I'm here alone."

"And you have a right to be," he agreed. "Mr. Collins watched you for a moment before he went in. We stood by the edge of the cliff and had an excellent view of all this area. He asked me to extend his compliments."

"Thanks," she said, genuinely pleased. "I was afraid he might still be annoyed at me."

"Not at all," Benjamin Willard assured her. "You really mustn't mind his moods. He's not a young man anymore and he's not at all well."

"I hope the change here will do him good."

Benjamin sighed. "It was a pilgrimage he had to make. I can't offer much hope for his condition. The doctors felt it a miracle he lived through his last seizure. The next one will probably be fatal."

"I'm sure you'd miss him a great deal," she said. "I understand you've been with him for years."

Benjamin Willard stared glumly down at the sand with its mixture of pebbles and sharp stones. "I'm devoted to him, miss. Make no mistakes about that. I've known him since his youth."

"The days of the Ritz Hampton Hotel?"

He nodded. "Back as far as that. So you are quite right. I shall be lost when death takes my employer."

Victoria was touched by the deep melancholy of his tone. "He is certainly lucky to have someone like you," she said. "And you are no longer a young man. It would be difficult for you to find another such position now. But I imagine he will see that you are generously provided for."

"I expect he will remember me in his will," he agreed.

Anxious to change the subject, she went on, "I hear you have made a study of astronomy."

The elderly man stared out at the horizon with a pleased expression on his lined face. "I have spent some interesting hours at it in the last ten years or so. I've a telescope set up on the captain's walk."

"I noticed you were up there last night."

"It offers a splendid view." He turned to her. "Would you care to come up and see the equipment after you've dressed?"

She nodded. "I'd like to very much."

"Fine," he said. "I'm going straight up there now. You'll have time to take a brief glimpse of things before lunch."

"I'll go up there from my room," she suggested. "It's on the top floor."

"I'll wait for you," he promised. And with a friendly nod he strode back up toward the path again.

When she joined him on the captain's walk, there was a light breeze blowing. It had come up at noon, as it so often did. Benjamin kept a hand on his panama hat to protect it from being blown away.

Victoria looked around at the wide expanse of scenery offered by this vantage point. The town seemed just a short distance off. Dotted here and there were the neighboring houses and the roads seemed narrow gray bands from so far above.

She said, "Just to stand up here and look around is worthwhile."

Benjamin smiled. "I quite agree. The stars were wonderful last night." He patted the large telescope mounted on a tripod. "This brought them very close. You can judge by focusing it on the village."

And he swung it around for her to study Collinsport through it.

She peered through the powerful instrument and gasped. "It's amazing," she said. "I can even read the signs on some of the buildings."

"It's a fine glass," Benjamin agreed happily. "I'll bet old Jeremiah Collins would have found use for it. He followed the sea, you know."

"Yes," she agreed, swinging the telescope and studying the countryside, "I've been told about him. And about this hill on which he built." She looked up from the telescope. "Did you know they called it Widow's Hill because it was where the fishermen's wives used to come and watch for the boats to appear on the horizon after a storm? When a boat failed to show up it was a signal that it had been lost and some of them would be widowed."

"Making a living along this coast has always been a cruel, rugged business," Benjamin agreed. And changing the subject, "I hope to make observations here tonight."

"I'd like to join you up here some night," she said.

"I'd be glad to have you," he replied.

"Is Mr. Collins interested in your hobby?"

Benjamin Willard shook his head. "My employer is a strange man, not much impressed by the technical advances of mankind. In fact, he disapproves of many of them. But he does show an interest in the stars in a rather different way."

"Oh?"

"He is interested in astrology. I believe he is convinced our fates are determined by the stars."

She smiled at the tall old man. "You don't share those beliefs?"

He shrugged and touched the telescope with a gnarled hand. "Let us say I am more attracted to the scientific aspect of the stars. Yet it is hard to tell. Believers in astrology may have some claim for their convictions. I have lived long enough to admit there are mysterious forces in the universe of which we are not aware."

Victoria offered him a skeptical smile. "Now you sound as if you might be hinting at a belief in ghosts!"

His gaunt face offered a study. "Perhaps I am."

"I find it hard to accept the idea of phantoms," she said, "even in surroundings such as we have here. And surely Collins House does hark back to the past."

"Indeed it does," he said solemnly.

"Still I am sure there are, as you say, many things we don't fully understand. Perhaps ghosts among them. Henry Collins seems a haunted type." She paused to smile briefly again. "I mean the way he clings to the past and that room."

Benjamin nodded. "You are quite right. He is haunted by a past that is perhaps more real to him than the present."

"And how do you feel about that?"

"I would prefer not to offer an opinion."

"I'm sorry," she said, "that was a stupid question." And she prepared to start down the stairs again.

"I've enjoyed our talk, miss," Benjamin Willard told her.

After lunch she took the station wagon in to Collinsport to do some errands for Elizabeth. One of them involved leaving a small suitcase for Carolyn at the bus station to be sent on by the afternoon bus to Bar Harbor. Each week her mother sent Carolyn a fresh supply of clothes. Victoria missed the spirited young girl who had come to seem almost like a sister to her. But Carolyn was enjoying her work and was not likely to return until the vacation season was over.

Having delivered the suitcase, Victoria went on to the large general store owned by the Collins Packing Company. It was located on the hilly main street of the fishing village and was one of the few old-fashioned stores of its type left in that part of Maine. Its long counters held a wealth of articles from tacks to tents. And the cool, gloomy interior of the old shop offered a fascinating odor compounded of all the variety of its merchandise from leather goods to open casks of sweet pickles.

As a city girl, Victoria still found it an experience to shop there and she spent a leisurely half-hour selecting the goods listed by Elizabeth. A short-sleeved clerk then carried the items out to the station wagon. As it was still too early to go home, she drove down to the wharf and parked, thinking she might see Joe Haskel, Carolyn's fisherman boyfriend.

But there was no sign of him, although a few of the fishing boats were tied up there. She was about to get back into the station wagon when a sleek white convertible drove up close beside her and Burke Devlin got out from behind its wheel to greet her. The mystery man of Collinsport was wearing white slacks and a blue shirt open at the neck. He was bronzed from the summer sun and appeared quite young and handsome.

"Hello!" he said. "Where have you been keeping yourself?"

She smiled. "We have guests at Collins House."

"Really?" He offered her a teasing look. "Ernest among them?"

Victoria blushed and shook her head. "No. It's Mr. Henry Collins, Elizabeth's uncle, and his party."

Burke whistled softly. "Old Henry Collins! I didn't know he was still alive."

"He hasn't been well," she admitted. "And he's very old."

"I'd think so," Devlin said. "He's a kind of spooky old boy, isn't he?"

She smiled. "Strange, but really very nice. He seems to live almost completely in the past. There is a room in the house that interests him."

Burke Devlin's expression showed that he had heard about the hidden room. And he said, "Collins House has its share of surprises, hasn't it?"

"Yes. So you know about that special room."

"A little," he said. "As I understand it the old man had it rebuilt exactly as it was in a famous New York hotel."

"You should see it," she said. "It's fascinating."

"I doubt that I will," Burke said dryly. "Especially if I depend on Roger for an invitation."

"I'm sure Elizabeth would be glad to have you any time," Victoria assured him. "And I hear you're interested in some construction yourself. That you are building the big new house out at the corner."

His eyebrows raised. "Who told you that?"

"Roger mentioned it at the dinner table the other night."

Burke Devlin smiled grimly. "You should know by now Roger Collins is not a reliable authority where I'm concerned."

"You aren't directly denying you're building the house," she pointed out.

"We'll go into that another time," he said. "When are you coming back to the village again?"

She sighed. "I don't know. With Carolyn away I don't come in much. But I'll be back again some evening soon."

"I'll see you then," he promised. "You can find me at the hotel or the Blue Whale. I never stray far from the regular places."

"But when you do stray, you do it on a grand scale," she said, referring to his occasional journeys on business to other parts of the world.

He gave her one of his mysterious smiles. "Just now my main interest happens to be Collinsport," he said.

They talked a few minutes longer and then each of them got in their cars and drove away. Victoria took the narrow, hilly road that led to Collins House and it was not too late in the afternoon when she got back there. Not wanting to bother the sullen Matt Morgan, she carried the various parcels into the house herself. The things for the refrigerator she carefully put inside it, since Elizabeth was not around. It was usual for her to take an afternoon nap at this time of day. Her work finished, she started upstairs to her own room.

As she reached the first floor landing Benjamin Willard appeared. The old man showed surprise and pleasure at seeing her. Coming forward, he said, "I've been looking for you all afternoon,

Miss Winters. Mr. Collins wants to see you."

"Oh?" she asked. "Is it urgent?"

The old man smiled discreetly. "He seems to think so, miss. When he gets an idea in his head he can be very impatient. If you have a free moment now I'd appreciate your giving it to him."

"Very well," she said. As she followed Benjamin down the cool, dark corridor leading to the apartment she wondered what the summons might mean. Perhaps it was merely that the old man wanted to apologize for his anger of the previous night.

Benjamin led her directly to the closet entrance of the crimson and ivory room. When they entered, Henry Collins was slumped in an easy chair before the great marble fireplace with his eyes closed.

Benjamin coughed quietly and the old man in the chair at once came awake. Then the servant said, "I've found Miss Winters."

Henry Collins raised himself up from the chair with effort, a smile crossed his worn face. "Ah, yes, Victoria. It was good of you to come."

"I've been in the village," she explained. "I just returned."

"Of course," Henry said, and then with a somewhat irritable glance at Benjamin who had remained standing there, he added, "I don't need you at the moment, Benjamin. You may go."

"You're sure, sir?" The old man hesitated, seeming reluctant to go.

"Quite sure!" Henry snapped.

Benjamin bowed his head slightly and turned and went out of the room. Henry Collins waited until he had gone. His face clouded with annoyance, he went over and shut the door and slid the bolt in it. He then turned to Victoria.

"Now we may be able to have a moment of privacy," he said.

She was puzzled by his conspiratorial air and the trouble he was taking to make sure they wouldn't be disturbed. Now she watched as he crossed the carpet slowly to the rolltop desk and unlocked it. Sliding the covering back, he rummaged inside and finally drew a small velvet-covered box out. He turned to her with the box in his hand.

"I have something for you," he said. "Something I want you to have. But no one must know about it."

"I don't understand," she said.

"You will," the old man told her, coming closer. He seemed more like a wraith than a human as he stood there in the shadowed room. "I hope this will help to make up for my unhappy anger last night," he said. And as he finished speaking he opened the velvet box to reveal a magnificent emerald pendant, with matching earrings and bracelet. It took only a glance to tell her they must be worth a small fortune!

Victoria was dumbfounded at the display of rich gems. After staring at them a moment, she said, "I couldn't accept a gift like that!"

"But you must," the old man urged. "I insist!"

"They're much too expensive!"

"Don't think about the expense," Henry Collins told her. "They have waited all these years for the proper person to wear them. And now they shall be yours!"

She looked at him with perplexed eyes. "Why?" she asked.

"One minute," he said, a look of delight on his patrician face. He placed the velvet box on a table nearby and lifted the shimmering green pendant and with trembling hands fastened it around her neck. Then he stood back a step studying her. "Yes," he said, as if talking to himself, "yes, just as it should be."

Victoria was growing more uneasy and confused all the time. The contrast of the old man's present mood with his anger of the night before convinced her he was not in a sound mental state. Yet he seemed to know what he was doing and he was definite enough in his convictions.

Staring at her sadly, he said, "I can guess what you're thinking. You're certain I must be a little mad." He raised a protesting hand. "Don't deny it! Not dangerously mad, but just senile."

She lifted her fingers to the pendant. "Surely you must know I can't take this or the other pieces from you."

"Wait a minute," he said. And taking her by the hand he led her over to one of the closet doors. He opened it to reveal a full length mirror on its inside. Making her stand before it so she could see herself and the precious gem he had hung at her neck, he asked, "Well?"

Studying herself in the mirror, she said, "It is lovely. Thank you for allowing me to see it."

He closed the door and faced her with a grave expression on his lined features. "My dear child," he said. "There are things I cannot reveal at this moment. Things I will explain later. You are entitled to these jewels."

"Entitled?"

"The pendant as well as the bracelet and earrings once belonged to a girl I loved with all my heart. A girl who was no stranger to this room."

Victoria was still puzzled. "How am I involved?"

He lifted a thin hand in protest. "Don't ask me that yet. Only let me tell you that you resembled her to such a remarkable degree that you could even be related!"

His emphasis on the word related made her heart leap. Was she at last on the way to discovering the secret of her identity? She had always felt that she must belong to some branch of the Collins family and now it appeared that this old man might corroborate her belief and sooner or later reveal the truth about her birth. It all fitted in. This must be why she had been brought here in the first place.

Her face brightening, she asked, "Am I really that much like her?"

Henry Collins stood staring at her in the soft light of the errant rays of the afternoon's fading sun. "You take me back half a century, just standing there wearing that pendant," he said, his eyes glowing with the happy memory of that other time. "I feel myself back in the Ritz Hampton Hotel. Just outside is Broadway, a Broadway such as you have never known. Hansom cabs and wagons, an occasional touring car, the trolleys clanging by and women in their long dresses and wide-brimmed hats, men in spats and homburgs." The old man's face was radiant as he ended his account and paused. "I feel I could close my eyes and again be part of that world of fifty years ago, so clearly do I recall it."

Victoria saw that this remembering had stirred the old man to the uttermost depths of his being. In a very real sense, she decided, what Benjamin had said to her about the hidden room being crowded with ghosts was right. The murky crimson and ivory room was filled with the spirits of those long dead, conjured up by Henry Collins' memory.

In a quiet voice, she said, "I'm sure it must have been a happy time for you."

The radiance left the old man's face. He sighed and she saw his hands clench. "It was both the happiest period of my life and the end of all the happiness I was to know."

There was a moment of silence in the high-ceilinged room. The light faded as the sun's rays were shut off from the window. The quick change had the eerie effect of a shadow crossing the room. She remembered that other afternoon when she had come into the empty room and smelled that delicate fragrance of perfume. Had a shadow crossed the room then as well? The shadow of some beautiful creature now many years a pitiful heap of dust?

Something outside her seemed to take control. An odd chill surged through her slender body, like the chill she thought must be associated with death. And then, very softly, she said, "She died, didn't she? This girl whom I resemble."

He nodded. "Yes. She died."

Victoria said, "And because you loved her so much and I remind you of her, you want to make me this extravagant gift?"

Henry Collins looked at her, and certainly his was a haunted expression. "You must accept the emeralds," he said. "I will tell you the rest of the story at another time. Then you will know you have done right."

Her thoughts quickened. Surely he was now telling her that the jewels were hers by right of inheritance. She knew little of his marriage beyond the fact that he had been married. Yet now she began to suppose he must have had a son or daughter and she was his grandchild. If only he would say it openly, what a difference it would make!

"You are expecting a great deal of me," she faltered. "Asking me to have so much faith in you!"

"It will only be a short time until you know everything," he said in a sad voice. "You realize I haven't long to live."

"Please!" she protested.

"But it is a fact we both must face. In the meantime I want you to take these and keep them in some hidden place. Tell no one about them."

Victoria frowned. "Not even Elizabeth?"

"I'm sorry," the old man said. "This must be our very own secret. You mustn't even tell Elizabeth." Moving close to her, he gently unhooked the pendant and took it from her neck. Then he put it in the velvet box with the other jewels and handed it to her.

She accepted the box hesitantly. "I don't know! Even after what you've hinted I'm not sure I have the right to these."

"You may be sure!"

"They could be stolen from me."

"Put them in a safe place."

"But when can I bring them into the open?"

He looked into her eyes. "Only after my death," he said. "There is a reason for that too. You will understand later." He moved across to a table on which a square cabinet rested. Turning to her, he said, "One more thing, before you leave."

She frowned. "Yes?"

"I want you to hear her."

Victoria's eyes widened. "The girl you loved? The dead girl?"

Henry Collins smiled sadly. "Don't look so astonished. We had the gramophone even in those long distant days. I have this one record. Very few know about it." He lifted the top off the walnut cabinet to reveal an old-fashioned cylinder record player. A round blue cylinder was in place. He flicked a switch and the needle engaged the record and it began to play.

There was no loud burst of music from the ancient machine. The voice that sang "Sweethearts" was eerily thin and sweet in a tragic way. A tinkling piano served as background for the girl's voice and the effect was much like that of some music-box with an unworldly air about it.

Henry Collins stood motionless for the entire length of the record, an intent expression on his patrician face as they stared at the revolving cylinder that held the only remaining link with that lost one of long ago. How many times must he have played the record over the years? How much heartbreak had the eerily sweet voice brought him? There were questions Victoria yearned to ask. What had happened to the girl? Had she and Henry Collins been married? Was there a child? And had that child been one of the parents she had never known? But she knew it would be useless. The old man had no intention of telling her any more at this point.

The record ended with a click. He snapped off the switch and replaced the cover of the walnut cabinet. Then he turned to her. With a sigh, he said, "That song was all the rage in 1916."

"She sang it very well."

The old man shrugged. "It would be hard for you to judge. Just a shadow of her true voice is on that record. I hope it was enough for you to guess her real talent."

"Did she sing on the stage?"

"For a time," he said. "I'm afraid I didn't approve. But that is another story." He came to her and took her free hand. "Victoria, I depend on you to keep this a secret as I have asked."

She swallowed hard. "Very well," she said.

He leaned close and touched his lips to her forehead. It was a gentle kiss, perhaps the kiss of a grandfather. At least that was what she hoped as he saw her out of the room. She kept the velvet jewel case concealed in the shopping bag she'd been carrying. It was all like part of some weird dream.

# CHAPTER 4

WHEN VICTORIA reached her room she realized she was faced with the difficult task of finding a hiding place for the emeralds. The old man had insisted they must be kept concealed until after his death. She stood glancing about her room with a puzzled frown on her pretty face. And then she recalled the loose board she had accidentally come upon in the ceiling of the room's single closet when she had been cleaning it out one day. The board could be raised and there was enough space to slip a good-sized box through. It would rest there on top of the other ceiling boards.

But at once she thought of rats. There were some in the old house; they might tear the soft velvet-covered case to tatters and make off with the jewels. Then she remembered a tin biscuit box she had received at Christmas from young David Collins. It had a hinged lid and would be just the thing for an outer cover for the jewel case. It took her some time to find it, place the other case in it, and hide them carefully away before replacing the board. When it was done she was satisfied no one would ever guess she had something hidden there.

The rest of the day and evening proved uneventful. She did not see Henry Collins again for several days. But the next morning while she was out in the garden picking a bouquet of flowers for the living room, Benjamin Willard came out to join her. The gaunt-faced old man was wearing his usual gray suit and panama hat.

He smiled at her and said, "I see you have many jobs."

Victoria paused in her task to look up at him. "This is one I especially like."

"I can well believe that. And what unusually good weather for Maine!"

"Don't let Elizabeth hear you speaking lightly of our weather," she said. "She thinks Maine has the best climate in the world."

"That's to be understood," the old man said. "But I have been here other summers with Mr. Collins when we've had rain for a week at a time. And it was cold!"

"It could happen again," Victoria admitted as she added some roses to her growing bouquet. "I've known times like that in my short stay here."

Benjamin glanced back at the towering old house. "What a pity that Mrs. Stoddard won't come out here to enjoy the fresh air and sunshine!"

"She seems to manage very well," Victoria said, keeping busy. It was a touchy subject which she would have preferred to avoid.

"Twenty years of confinement within those walls," the old man went on, his eyes still fixed on Collins House. "And by her own wish! Her own will!"

"She is a person of strong character," Victoria agreed.

Benjamin turned to her again. "But is it not something more than that?" he suggested. "I mean it goes beyond a question of character. Wouldn't you call it an example of eccentricity? An eccentric strain that is prominent in all the Collins family."

Victoria knew the old man was working around to something, but she couldn't be sure what it was. She said, "I'm not well enough acquainted with all of the family to pass that kind of judgment."

"Well, at least you have met my employer. And how can you not say that Henry Collins is a trifle mad? This business about the room! An insane obsession if I've ever seen one. Surely you must agree."

She stood up, holding her flowers. The aroma from the lovely bouquet filled her nostrils. She stared at Benjamin with incredulous eyes. "Are you suggesting Henry Collins is mad?"

"Close to it. There are all the signs." He paused rather awkwardly. "You must have noticed how secretive he is becoming. The way he dismissed me yesterday and insisted on being alone with you."

"I'd call that normal enough. He wanted to talk to me about some family matters. Perhaps he preferred you wouldn't hear. As it developed, he did confide in me more than I'd expected."

Benjamin raised his eyebrows. "Really?"

Victoria nodded. "So you see he did have a valid reason for wanting to be left alone with me. I hope he feels better for our having talked."

"He appears to be in good spirits today," Benjamin said.- "I trust he didn't talk a lot of nonsense. Make much of nothing."

Victoria was again surprised by the old man's words. She could see that he was trying to find out what Henry Collins had said to her. And she recalled how annoyed Benjamin had been at being sent out of the room. Henry had practically had to force him to leave. And now he was curious about what had gone on in his absence. Well, he would have to continue being curious. She was not going to break Henry Collin's confidence.

She said, "What he told me had the ring of truth. Beyond that I don't care to discuss it."

"Naturally not," Benjamin said affably. "Please don't get the impression I have been trying to pry. That is not my type."

"I'm sure of it," she said politely, although she felt the exact opposite to be true. She had the feeling he might know about the gift she'd received.

"You've done my employer a lot of good," Benjamin continued. "He seems to be taking an interest in you. That might turn out to be very valuable to you."

"I like him," she said. "I've enjoyed our few talks."

Benjamin smiled again. "I'll be happy to report your comment, miss. It is bound to cheer him up and can do you no harm."

"If you like," she said. "Will you please excuse me? I want to get these inside." And she hurried up the gravel walk toward the house, relieved to get away from Benjamin. He was in an odd frame of mind. She had not liked his attempting to discover what had gone on between her and Henry Collins.

As she entered the hallway, the first person she met was Benjamin's daughter-in-law. Molly Willard was in a shapeless house dress of some vague blue design and looking as jaded and dull-eyed as ever.

Nodding toward the garden, she said, "I saw you talking to the old man."

"Yes," Victoria said. "I like to talk to Mr. Willard."

Molly snorted. "Pompous old windbag! He's been with that Henry Collins so long he forgets he's a servant and thinks he's the old man's equal."

"They do get on well. They've been so long together."

"Too long, if you ask me," Molly said with a disgusted expression. "Me and Jack shouldn't have come down here. We could have got better jobs by staying in New York."

"But Mr. Collins does need you," Victoria said. "And you are doing your husband's father a favor by remaining on the job. I'm sure Mr. Willard appreciates it."

"If he does, it's the first time he's ever appreciated anything we've done for him," the drab woman said. "I could tell you stories if I wanted to that would make those flowers wilt."

Victoria was puzzled by her vehemence. "You sound very upset," she said.

"I am upset," Molly Willard said, "and with good reason. Now Jack is hanging around out in that garage with Matt Morgan and drinking. Morgan always has liquor with him."

"I hadn't realized," she said.

Molly gave her a scathing glance and started toward the stairs. As she took the first step she turned, to say, "There's a lot of things you haven't realized. And the sooner your eyes are opened, the better for you, I say. Why don't you ask old Henry or Benjamin to tell you the real story behind that hidden room!" Molly quickly went on upstairs.

Again Victoria was left wondering. She went on to the kitchen to fill a vase with water and arrange the flowers. Elizabeth was working at the stove and glanced around to see who it was.

"Flowers!" Elizabeth exclaimed. "I'm glad you thought of them. We should send a bunch up to Uncle Henry too!"

"This is a large bunch," she said. "Perhaps we could divide it and send half of them to him."

"A good idea," Elizabeth said. "You put them in two vases and as soon as I finish here I'll take one of them upstairs myself."

As Victoria worked at the flowers she went over what Molly had said and tried to think it all out. Molly was plainly not too intelligent and so it would be wrong to take her words too seriously. Yet there was no mistaking her feeling of hatred toward her father-in-law. And she had made a dark reference to the hidden room and the explanation behind it.

Meanwhile Victoria was stubbornly holding to her belief that she was at least a distant member of the Collins family. She wouldn't want to find herself too closely related or that might spoil her romance with Ernest Collins and she did not want that to happen. But if she had only some kinship with the family and could prove it and discover who her parents were she'd be satisfied. Or at least she felt she would.

Casually she asked Elizabeth, "Was Henry Collins married?"

"Yes," her employer said from the stove. "Why do you ask?"

"He seems so alone. He would be so much better off if he had a wife to share his old age."

"I guess that wasn't meant to be," Elizabeth said with a sigh. "She died young, I understand."

Victoria tried hard to sound casual. "Did they have any children?"

"Yes, I believe so," Elizabeth said vaguely, as if her mind was on something else. She came over to the table and took one of the vases filled with flowers. "This is a nice one. I'll take it upstairs now," she said. And before Victoria could say anything else to her, she was on her way out of the kitchen.

It left her with her most important questions unanswered. Had Elizabeth deliberately timed her exit to avoid giving her more information? It seemed that whenever Victoria came up with some truly pertinent questions, the mistress of Collins House found a way to avoid answering them.

She felt so strongly on this that she tried to see Henry Collins later in the day. But at the door of the apartment Benjamin Willard met her and informed her she couldn't speak with the old man as he was resting.

"He's not ill?" she asked anxiously.

"Not really," Benjamin said, an odd expression on his gaunt face. "But he is far from well and needs every bit of rest he can get."

"I wouldn't want to disturb him," she said. "Perhaps he'll be free to see me later."

"Possibly," Benjamin said. "But I wouldn't count on it. He's very much in a mood today. Depressed, is what I mean."

"I see," she said slowly. "Well, thanks, anyway."

"Not at all, miss," Benjamin said with cold politeness.

As she walked back along the corridor to the main part of the house she realized that Benjamin had been almost openly hostile to her. At first she wondered why and then she remembered their talk in the garden. He was apparently angry at her because she had held back the information concerning her talk with Henry Collins. The old man had bound her to secrecy and she had no intention of violating her promise to him.

Yet now Benjamin was against her and would probably continue to make it difficult for her to see and talk with the old man. She began to wonder if there wasn't something sinister about the old man which had escaped her before. Was he a malevolent force in her grandfather's life and had he played some dark role in the drama that had condemned the hidden room to being a place of tragic memories?

Depressed at the atmosphere of the bleak old house, she had an urge to go to the village for a while in the evening. Elizabeth readily gave her permission to use the station wagon for the evening and shortly after eight o'clock she headed for Collinsport. She was really going to have a talk with Burke Devlin. Her respect for him had grown with their friendship. And now that she was filled with a mixture of conflicting emotions, she needed his kindly advice.

It was twenty after eight when she parked at the hotel and went into the coffee shop. The girl behind the counter said, "Mr. Devlin left about a half-hour ago. Said he was going to the Blue Whale."

Victoria nodded her thanks. "I'll find him," she said. She supposed she would start wagging tongues by going around looking for Burke Devlin, but at this point she didn't much care.

The neon lights of the Blue Whale were already on by the time she parked her car on the side street close to it. The big ramshackle building in which the lounge was located was shabby looking. Its ancient clapboards were peeling paint and it seemed little like a glamor spot. Yet it offered Collinsport's only touch of nightlife and was always well patronized. Visitors and the younger set gathered there.

Victoria always drew within herself when she entered the noisy, smoke-filled spot. Loud talk and raucous laughter joined with the jukebox to make a constant clamor. Once in there awhile, one became deadened to the noise. The stools at the bar were filled and she made her way past the booths lining the side wall. Several couples were dancing at the far end by the jukebox and she spotted Burke Devlin sitting by himself in the next to the last booth, somehow managing to concentrate on the newspaper he held in front of him.

She slipped into the seat opposite him and said laughingly, "You surely must have mastered the art of concentration!"

"An old yogi secret," he said, smiling as he put the newspaper aside. "I was also indulging in another yogi practice. Willing that some lovely young maiden would come and join me. And here you are!"

"Not by your magic," she rebuffed him. "A little sorcery of my own. I talked Elizabeth into letting me have the station wagon."

"Anyway, you arrived." After inquiring what she would like, he ordered for them from the waitress who had come over to the booth.

Victoria looked around. "It's just as quiet as always," she said.

"The noise offers complete privacy," Burke Devlin said with quiet amusement. "It's the only place like it in town. Unique!"

"You haven't seen Carolyn's boyfriend here tonight?"

He shook his head. "No. Does he usually come in every evening?"

"It's the village gathering place," Victoria said. "But he may have driven over to Bar Harbor to see Carolyn." The waitress came with their orders and left them again.

Burke gave her a penetrating glance. "You seem very much on edge tonight."

She smiled. "I am. I had to talk to someone. How's this for a start? I think I may be a Collins."

He arched an eyebrow. "Really?"

"Uh-huh! What do you say to that?"

"I'm not sure it's anything to be excited about," he said with a smile. "And particularly not if you're seriously interested in Ernest

Collins as you claim to be. That would make you relatives."

She shook her head. "So distant it wouldn't matter."

"I see," he said. "And what brought on this sudden brainstorm?"

"You remember my telling you about Elizabeth's Uncle Henry?"

"Yes."

"I've talked to him a good deal since he arrived. He's a pathetic, charming old man." She paused. "And he seems especially fond of me. I've never had a comparative stranger take such an interest in me before."

"And you think there is some special reason for his show of interest?"

She nodded. "I'm almost sure of it. Little things he's said. A gift he's made me and a promise he's asked me to keep. I'd like to tell you more, but I can't without breaking my word to him."

Burke Devlin looked a little short of pleased. He eyed her gravely. "So he's given you a gift and made you some promises as well as binding you to secrecy?"

"Yes. You sound as if there was something wrong in that?"

"Don't you think it a little strange?"

Victoria frowned. "He's trying to be nice to me. Perhaps make up for the things I've never known. It could even turn out that I'm his granddaughter."

The handsome man across from her sighed. "I hate to see you building on it so much, Victoria. You might be opening yourself to a great deal of hurt."

"You don't think I am related to him?" Her tone was plaintive.

"How can I answer that without upsetting you?" he asked. "You must see you've gotten yourself in a state over this business already."

Victoria saw what he meant. It was true she was allowing her hopes to run high. And now that she had found someone to whom she could talk freely, she had expressed her deepest feelings on the matter. But if these things weren't true, why would the old man have given her that valuable jewelry and said what he had? It was a confusing and troubling question. She didn't dare explain to Burke Devlin the nature of the gift, which might make him see it all differently.

She said, "As usual, you've given me good advice. I shouldn't count on this too much." Her voice was low with unhappiness.

"I'm sorry to bring these things to your attention," Burke said. "But it's part of the difficult role of being a friend. Often you have to hurt those you are fondest of by being frank."

"I understand," she said, studying her glass.

"I've always felt you put too much emphasis on the possibility of being related to the Collins family, anyway," he said. "One day you may find the real clue to your parents and it could surprise you."

She looked up at him with sad eyes. "I've waited a long time."

"So you should have learned patience," he said with another of his smiles. "In the meantime, don't get too involved with this Henry Collins. I've been making some inquiries from the older men in the village about him. They all agree he's a very strange member of a strange family."

Her eyes widened. "Just what does that mean?"

"Those I talked to remember him coming here first as a young man. He was a sort of dandy; his fancy manners and natural charm made him popular. He was sought out for all the parties in the area. Then he married and brought his wife back for several summers in succession. She was a pretty girl and they both entered fully in the lively summer social life of the community. After that there was a break of nearly ten years. And when Henry Collins returned he came with only his servant, Benjamin, for company and never left Collins House. He had become a recluse in the period he was away. And he has been one in all the years since."

She listened with serious interest. "It must have been in that interval his wife died. I believe he loved her a great deal."

"That might explain it," Burke Devlin agreed. "However, I warn you, the theory in the village is that he became slightly demented."

"I don't think there is anything wrong with his mind," Victoria said stoutly. But at the same time she remembered Benjamin's warning about his employer's mental state.

She talked a little longer with Burke and then he saw her to her car and she drove back to the lonely house on the ocean's edge. Only a single light showed and it was in the lower hallway. Otherwise the old mansion was dark and silent.

She made her way quickly up the stairs, aware of every creak from the groaning old wood. When she reached the third floor she found it also in darkness. The small night light had probably burned out and she would have to replace it in the morning. She reached her door and opening it groped for the light switch. But she didn't find it!

Because her attention was caught by a frightening apparition standing in the center of her room. Faintly visible in the light from the window was the figure of a woman in a dress of long ago. While she stared at the ghostly creature, she was at the same time aware of a faint scent of that familiar haunting perfume!

# CHAPTER 5

V ICTORIA STOOD in the doorway of the room for a long
moment frozen with horror. By the murky light filtering in
through the window she could just make out a vague outline of
the phantom creature. The woman seemed tallish and wore a long,
flowing dress with pinched waist and full bosom. On her head
was a wide-brimmed hat, the veil of which covered her face. It was
impossible to make out her features. She came slowly across in an
almost floating motion to where Victoria stood.

The sight of this strange apparition coming gradually nearer
proved too much for Victoria's already highly-strung nerves. With
a cry of alarm she turned and fled from the room to the head of
the stairs. There she paused for a moment in the darkness of the
landing and screamed again. And then she ran down the steps to
the next floor where the dim night bulb in its side wall fixture gave
at least some dull illumination.

Almost the moment she reached the lower landing
Elizabeth appeared in the corridor in her dressing gown. The older
woman showed concern as she hurried to join her.

"I heard you scream twice," she said. "What is wrong?" And
she glanced up the shadowed stairway.

Tears brimmed in Victoria's eyes. "In my room," she gasped.
"I saw something! A woman dressed in old-fashioned clothes, sort

of floating there in the shadows! A kind of phantom figure!"

Elizabeth's eyes opened wide and she placed a comforting arm around her. "You've obviously had a bad scare," she said. "But you mustn't be panicked by what was probably only the window curtain blowing in the night wind."

Gradually regaining her poise, Victoria shook her head. "No," she protested. "It wasn't something I imagined. I really did see some kind of figure up there!"

The older woman sighed deeply with her arm still around her. "There has been far too much talk about the past and tragedy lately," she said. "It has upset you."

Victoria glanced fearfully toward the stairs leading to the third floor. "She was waiting there for me in my room!"

Elizabeth patted her shoulder comfortingly. "Now don't talk about it so much," she said. "You will convince me as well as yourself you saw a ghost. And I'm sure it was some sort of illusion."

"No!"

"I'll go upstairs with you now and we'll see what we find," Elizabeth said with a reassuring smile. "The best policy is to at once track down these supposed specters. My experience has been they usually turn out to be something much less alarming."

Victoria began to feel embarrassed in the face of the older woman's calm. It could be that she had let her nerves get out of hand and made herself ridiculous. So much had happened in the past few days. She had been so overwhelmed by the atmosphere of the hidden room and the nostalgic reminiscences of old Henry Collins. Yet she was certain she had seen the woman she had described—and there had been that elusive aroma of the perfume!

As they started up the stairs she felt herself trembling a little and in a tight voice she told Elizabeth, "I shouldn't be bothering you this way so late at night."

"It's nothing," Elizabeth said. "Did you have a nice evening?"

"Yes." They were at the head of the stairs now and the silence of the dark landing made her so nervous she could not even concentrate enough to make conversation. Glancing down the shadowed corridor leading to her room, she was certain the ghostly figure must still be lurking there.

Elizabeth must have sensed her sudden panic. She said, "I'll go take a look first."

"I'll go with you!" She forced the words from her lips and stayed at Elizabeth's side as she went briskly down the dark hallway.

"A nuisance, the hall night light being out," Elizabeth said. "We must replace the bulb in the morning."

"Be careful!" Victoria warned her in a taut whisper as the older woman reached the entrance of her room.

Elizabeth made no reply as she went inside. A moment later the light was turned on and as Victoria hesitantly entered, Elizabeth turned to her with one of her warm smiles.

"You see!" She gestured with a slim hand. "Your phantom visitor!" And it did seem that she might be right. For a sudden night wind was fitfully blowing in through the half open window and billowing the long curtains in a wraith-like fashion.

She stood there reluctant to agree, yet knowing that she probably should. "I don't know," she faltered. "I could even make out the vague outline of the woman's figure and see the hat and veil she was wearing. She was dressed in the fashion of fifty years ago!"

Elizabeth lowered the window and pulled the curtains in place. Now turning to her, she smiled. "The more detailed your description, the more certain I am you've been drawing on your imagination. I think you've been letting Uncle Henry's stories and the magazines and newspapers in that museum room of his fill your head with a lot of nonsense."

"Not really," she said in a low voice.

"That blowing curtain could suggest any number of ghostly creatures in the darkness," Elizabeth said coming over to her. "I've always given you credit for a level head, Victoria. I hope you're not going to develop nerves at this late date."

"I'm sorry I brought you up here," she faltered, already regretting her quick actions and uncertain about what she had actually seen.

"Not at all. I'm glad to settle this. Now that you have a proper explanation for what happened I'm sure you won't think about it again."

"I'll try not to," she said.

Elizabeth went out into the corridor again and Victoria accompanied her to the head of the stairs. "Blame the missing light for most of it," Elizabeth said.

They were at the point of saying goodnight and Victoria was ready to return to her room, contrite and feeling she had caused an unseemly amount of commotion over nothing. And then as they stood there in the shadowed hallway there came a definite sound of someone moving in the darkness. They simultaneously glanced at each other and both stared into the shadows with fear on their faces.

The sound now resolved itself into footsteps coming nearer them. A board creaked and then from the shadows emerged the figure of Benjamin Willard. Seeing them, the old man came to a halt, looking startled.

"I hope I didn't alarm you ladies," he observed.

Elizabeth touched a hand to her throat and with a timorous smile, said, "You almost had us believing in ghosts, Mr. Willard."

"Is that a fact?" he said. "I'm sorry, indeed. I've been up on the roof with my telescope. I declare the heavens have never been brighter on a summer evening. But realizing the hour, I decided it was time I came back down to bed."

"I should have remembered about your being up there," Elizabeth said. "I'm glad it's turning out well."

Benjamin smiled. "I found myself a new star tonight and I'd say that's real progress. I plan to watch it for the next few nights and see if I can decide on its proper name." With a bow to them both, he went on down the steps.

Elizabeth gave her a reproving look after he'd vanished. "You had me in nearly as bad a state as yourself. So you see our second ghost was only poor old Benjamin."

"I was almost as frightened as before," she confessed.

"Because you've allowed yourself to get in a mental state to accept ghosts," the other woman reproved her. "Believe me, the majority of mysterious footsteps are nothing but weary old boards creaking in the night, the rustlings in deserted rooms are caused by mice or even squirrels, and the tapping on a window is usually caused by a bewildered June bug or bat!"

With this final dismissal of ghostly occurrences Elizabeth said goodnight and went on down to the floor below and her own room. Victoria, still not altogether herself, made her way slowly down the dark upper hallway and into the welcoming brightness of her own lighted bedroom. She turned the key in the lock before she began preparing for bed.

As she advanced to the small basin in the corner of the room her eye was caught by a tongue of silk protruding from the top of one of the dresser drawers. By the beige shade she recognized it as being a favorite slip of hers. She frowned at her carelessness in closing the drawer and then realized she hadn't worn that particular slip for weeks. In fact, she hadn't even opened that drawer for days!

But someone else had! With this thought leaping into her mind she went over to the dresser and pulled the offending drawer open. And she gave a small gasp of astonishment as she saw that its contents were in a jumbled mess! No wonder the slip had been caught as it had. Someone had made a hurried search of the drawer and left it in complete disorder.

It took her only a moment to check on the other drawer and the one at the bottom. In every case the result turned out to be identical. Someone had made a hasty search of the entire dresser.

Leaving behind the disorder, she hurried to the closet and threw the door open. She could tell that someone had been there, as well, by the way the dresses were pushed back. Many of them had been removed from the rod on which they hung and been replaced in a different order. Automatically her eyes went to the ceiling of the closet, her hiding place for the emeralds. No one had been up there. Her secret hiding place had turned out to be an excellent one.

With a worried expression she closed the closet door and turned to stare at the dresser. So she had not been so wrong after all! Someone had been in there and ransacked her room. But was this the work of a ghost? Or should she suspect Benjamin Willard, who had emerged from the shadows with the excuse he had been up on the roof?

Her suspicions of Benjamin fitted in with the unpleasant portrait she was gradually assembling of him. He had been strangely curious about her conversation with Henry Collins and tried to get information about it in every possible way. And he had behaved coldly when she'd refused to tell him anything. Had he found out about the emeralds anyway and come searching for them? Or was it that the emeralds had attracted the spirit of the lovely girl who had once worn them?

Either solution would be an unhappy one and she was well aware there could be some other answer of which she was completely ignorant. Sadly she went about straightening out the dresser drawers and when she finished began getting ready for bed.

She encountered Roger at breakfast for the first time in several days. He usually came down later than she did and ate while she was out in the kitchen with Elizabeth. This morning he bustled into the dining room early.

"Important meeting of the directors today," he informed her as he took his place at the table. Elizabeth prepared breakfast buffet style as she did the majority of meals and they each helped themselves. He took a sip of his orange juice and gave her a knowing glance. "I had no idea you preferred older men," he said.

She stared at him. "Why do you say that?"

He shrugged. "You seem charmed with the dubious virtues of Uncle Henry, for one thing."

"He seems a very nice old gentleman."

"Nice old fraud," Roger scoffed. "You'll find out about him."

Victoria frowned. "I don't think you're being fair."

"I happen to have known him for a lot longer time than you."

"Granted. But you're prejudiced and won't allow yourself to like him."

Roger poured cream on his cereal. "Now what do you see

him as? A fragile relic from another age, broken-hearted by the tragedy of a dead love and lost in the coldly foreign spirit of today. Is that the Henry Collins you imagine? A weak, sensitive old man, too gentlemanly to cope with the ugly world of reality and so building himself a cocoon of make-believe in his restored hotel room for protection?"

She smiled in spite of her slight annoyance. "You're becoming quite eloquent," she said.

"Unusual for me this early in the morning," he admitted. "But given a goodly number of martinis I can envelop you with rhetoric by dusk. Still you haven't offered me any answer. What sort of man do you believe Henry to be?"

She paused to consider. "A very nice person from another age," she said at last.

Roger eyed her bleakly across the table. "You couldn't be more wrong."

"I expected you to say something like that."

"It's part of your prejudice in favor of age," Roger continued slyly. "But I see by last night that you don't only prefer old men."

"Last night?"

"Last night in town, to be precise," he said, with a sarcastic smile. He was plainly enjoying himself.

She looked down at the half-finished piece of toast on her plate. "I don't know what you're talking about."

"But you must know who I'm talking about," he insisted. "Come now, you can't have forgotten that earnest conversation you had with Burke Devlin at the Blue Whale. You were concentrating on it so much neither of you saw me come in and take a seat at the bar."

"I certainly didn't," she said. "So you were spying on me?"

He laughed. "That's a strong word, Victoria. Collinsport is a small town and it's pretty hard to avoid bumping into people you know at every turn."

"It isn't too bad as long as people mind their own business," she said.

He spread his hands and sat back in his chair. "You know me! Live and let live is my motto! If you want to spend your time with a man like Burke it's up to you. I can't understand it, but as I say, it's up to you."

"I met Burke when I first came to Collinsport. We've been good friends ever since."

He poured himself coffee. "Is Burke really a good friend to anyone?"

"I can answer that for myself. Yes."

Roger looked glum. "You don't have much loyalty to us here,

do you?" he asked. "You know how it is between Burke and me."

"I don't see that it has anything to do with loyalty," Victoria declared firmly. "I have a right to choose my own friends. And Mrs. Stoddard has never objected."

He sipped his coffee. "Elizabeth wouldn't. But I doubt if Ernest would like it any more than I do if he knew about it."

"I've mentioned Burke in my letters to Ernest."

Roger looked a little brighter, as if he felt he'd found a weak spot in her defense. "But he doesn't know you're spending whole evenings with him."

"That doesn't mean anything."

"It would to me if I were in Ernest's place. I'll bet the gossips in the village are chattering about you and Devlin now."

Victoria stood up indignantly. "I've never heard anything so silly!"

He finished his coffee and grinned maliciously as he rose. "Don't think Ernest is above jealousy. Because he happens to be a famous musician doesn't mean he isn't human like the rest of us. You should at least be loyal to Cousin Ernest!" Roger was always at his nastiest when he referred to the young musician as Cousin Ernest. And Victoria always found it particularly annoying to hear him make the reference. He gave her no chance to make a reply, leaving the dining room at once.

As she gathered up the dirty dishes and began taking them out to the kitchen she considered what he had said. She knew she was being silly even to think twice about his snide remarks. And yet he had worried her. Was she in danger of creating a scandal by continuing her close friendship with Burke Devlin?

When she had washed up the breakfast things she sought out Elizabeth in her study. Elizabeth not only took care of running the household, she also kept a close check on the operations of the family fish-packing company. And often during the morning she worked at her desk in the book-lined study. She was sitting there intent on the typed sheets spread out before her when Victoria went in.

Raising her eyes from her work, she said, "Well, I hope you had a fair night's rest after all the excitement."

"I did manage to sleep fairly well," Victoria said with a smile.

"Good. You mustn't allow yourself to become so tense."

"I still think there was someone in my room," she said. "Most of the things in the dresser were upset. Someone must have come to my room searching for something."

Elizabeth frowned, looking very much the businesswoman sitting there. "Someone went through your things?"

"Yes."

"But why?"

"I don't know." She didn't dare mention the emeralds. Henry Collins had bound her to secrecy about them. For the time being she must go on as if they didn't exist.

"I can't imagine what the motive would be. The small amount of money you might keep up there wouldn't justify such an act."

"There was nothing missing," she confessed.

The older woman sighed. "One doesn't like to think of there being a sneak thief in the house."

She gave Victoria a level look. "On the other hand, we can't escape the fact we have some comparative strangers staying under our roof."

Victoria had an idea whom she meant. As Elizabeth spoke she pictured the brash Jack Willard, Henry's chauffeur. She wouldn't put it past Benjamin's son to steal if the opportunity presented itself.

She said, "It is hard to tell about people you don't know too well."

Elizabeth studied the papers on the desk grimly. "And one can't rely on Uncle Henry's judgment these days. He can't keep proper check on his people because he's much too ill and decrepit. I'm shocked by the change in him."

"I wouldn't notice it as you do, since I have no way of comparing his condition now with what he was like before."

The older woman looked up at her. "I can promise you it's frightening. I'm afraid he's a very sick man. I only hope he doesn't have a bad spell here with the nearest hospital in Ellsworth. For that reason also, I dislike talking to him about these problems."

"It may not happen again," Victoria said hopefully.

"I'd be very much upset if there were any recurrences," Elizabeth promised. "And depend on it, I'll keep a close eye on what is going on."

Victoria remained just long enough to receive instructions for the day from the older woman. Elizabeth wanted her to start the wash in the big automatic washer in the kitchen. This meant gathering the linen from upstairs. She left the study and went along the hallway to the front of the house. When she was almost there she heard Benjamin Willard and his son Jack coming down the stairs. By halting where she was, she could get a glimpse of them as they reached the hallway and made their way out the front door. They were arguing in such a low tone she couldn't make out their words. But there was no doubt in her mind the two men were quarreling.

Her first reaction was to wonder what they were arguing about. And then she realized with both men out of the way she might have a further chance to talk with Henry Collins alone and tell him about her room being ransacked the previous night. It was possible he might be able to guess who was responsible. She wouldn't say anything about the apparition she'd been so sure she'd seen—it would surely upset him, and Elizabeth had pretty well proven her ghost was merely a billowing window curtain.

Victoria hurried upstairs, aware that only one barrier might stand between her and seeing the old man in private: there was still the dowdy Molly Willard to be reckoned with. So it came as no surprise to her when she reached the end of the dark corridor joining the rear wing with the rest of the house to find the faded blonde seated in a chair in the living room, watching the ancient television set Elizabeth had put in there for her uncle's use.

When Victoria reached the doorway of the room, the blonde turned to stare at her. "You see my Jack anywhere?" she asked.

"Yes," Victoria said. "He and his father went down the stairs a little while ago. They went out someplace."

Molly looked bored and annoyed. "What does he mean running off on his own? I told him I wanted to go to the village. I got groceries and stuff to get."

"Perhaps he's just gone out to the garage," Victoria suggested.

Molly glared at her. "He'll probably not show up for hours. I know him!"

"Is Mr. Collins in the other living room?"

"If you mean that crazy old restored hotel room, he is. I swear he talks to himself in there. I hear talk and when I go in he's alone."

"Often the very old do that."

"You like the old coot, don't you?" Molly eyed her suspiciously.

"I find him interesting," she said. "I'd like to speak to him now. Is it all right if I knock on the door to the hidden room?"

"Go ahead. I don't guarantee he'll answer though." The woman turned away and began watching the television again. It was a cooking school and Victoria doubted if the woman had much interest in it beyond the fact that it provided something to watch.

Victoria went back along the hall and knocked on the door of the hidden room. After a moment Uncle Henry invited her in.

Opening the door, she saw him standing by the window looking out. When he saw her he seemed delighted and came over to meet her. She had closed the door after her.

He said, "I've been thinking about you, my dear."

"And I had to see you alone," she said. "There's something I want to tell you. Something to do with your gift."

The old man's patrician features clouded. "What are you saying?"

"Someone came to my room last night and went through all my things," she said. "They upset the whole place. My dresser was a mess." She paused. "So it must have leaked out in some way. Somebody must know I have the emeralds."

"But that can't be," he protested weakly. "I told no one. And I'm quite sure no one could have overheard us."

"Why else would they want to search my room?"

He shook his head. "I realize it's puzzling."

"Those emeralds must be worth a great deal."

The old man rubbed his chin. "Don't be too hasty reaching conclusions. Let me have time to think about this."

"Perhaps I should give them back to you," she suggested.

"Not yet!" He raised a protesting hand and looked so pathetic and shaky she hadn't any desire left to argue the matter. She felt he might be about to collapse and didn't want to feel responsible.

So she said, "Very well, I'll keep them. But it could mean placing me in danger."

"I don't want that," he said. "The very idea alarms me. But I think you're making too much of this."

Victoria stared at him intently. "Can't you tell me more about the emeralds and why you are so insistent I have them?"

His agitation increased. "Not yet!"

"Was there some dreadful tragedy connected with them and this room?"

It was his turn to stare at her. Fear showed in his eyes.

Then he turned away from her with a low moan. "Why do you ask that?"

"Because of a strange feeling that comes over me when I enter here."

"It's your imagination," he said, his back still to her. "This was a happy room once. That is why I cling to it and the memories it offers."

She knew by his strained voice and his manner that he wasn't being completely truthful. She also knew it was too much to expect from him. With a glance at the engraving above the fireplace, she said, "I suppose I must take your word for it."

Now he seemed to have recovered himself and he turned to her, seeming calmer. "You must come back again when we can talk without being overheard. I have some important things to think out. Later, I will tell you all that you want to know. You understand?"

"Perhaps. I'm not certain."

He patted her arm gently. "Good girl! I know I can depend on you." His eyes met hers; there was deep anxiety in them. "But you must take care. Protect yourself from the evil that surrounds us."

At that moment the door opened and Benjamin Willard came in. He made no apology for his intrusion. With a nod for Victoria, he addressed himself to Henry Collins. "Mrs. Stoddard has accepted your invitation to join you here for tea and she has asked you to be her dinner guest."

The old man nodded his white head. "Tell her I'll be delighted." And to Victoria, he added, "You are included in the tea invitation as well, my dear."

She smiled. "Thank you. I must get back to work or I won't be finished by then." She went out, knowing that she would learn nothing more with Benjamin there to hear every word.

Once again she felt the old man had been close to making some startling revelation and then drew away from it. Once again her hopes were raised. Surely he had meant she was a Collins—a blood relation of his and so entitled to the emeralds.

Thinking again of the robbery attempt, she wondered, in view of the old man's certainty that no one else knew of the emeralds, whether the jewels were really the motive for the intrusion. Could it be someone looking for a clue as to whether she was related to Henry Collins? Someone who had reason to suspect who she was and wanted to dispute the fact or prevent her from being recognized as kin to the old man?

When she returned to the kitchen with an armful of soiled linen, Elizabeth was standing by the washer waiting. She said, "I finished my work in the study and came out here. I couldn't imagine what was keeping you."

Victoria apologized, "I stopped to talk to your Uncle Henry a moment."

Elizabeth smiled as she took the clothes from her. "I might have known. He has an eye for pretty young girls even at his age. Did you hear we are invited to tea with him?"

"Yes. Benjamin came in while I was there. He also spoke to Mr. Collins about coming down here for dinner."

"Did he accept?"

"Yes. He seemed quite pleased."

"I'm glad," Elizabeth said as she finished placing the clothes and soap powder in the washer and closed the top. "He's so apt to shut himself up alone in that room. And it isn't good for him."

"You know, that room has a strange influence on me. Sometimes when I'm standing there I can sense an evil in it that almost sickens me."

Elizabeth started the washer and shaking her head said, "You have far too active an imagination."

"Don't you feel anything about that room at all?"

"I find it old and charming," the other woman said. "Isn't that enough?"

"I'd say you were fortunate," Victoria said. "I know I'm too sensitive."

Elizabeth smiled. "What you need is more fresh air and sunshine and less of this old house," she said. "I'm going to send you up to the field to pick some strawberries for tonight's dinner."

"I'd like that," she said.

"Then you can go right away," Elizabeth told her. "Take one of the quart cans. Fill it and we'll have enough. Matt Morgan told me the fields were red with them."

Victoria put on her sunglasses and the wide-brimmed straw hat she used when she would be exposed to the sun a lot. The day was humid, and she remembered that thundershowers had been predicted. Certainly there were no signs of them now. She walked the short distance to the field, which was about a mile from the estate grounds and off the road leading to the village.

While she picked, clouds formed. The sun went in for a few minutes at first, emerged again, and then went back behind the clouds for a longer period. It took her only a short time to fill the quart pail and then start back.

She had gone about a third of the distance along the narrow dirt road when she saw the car belonging to Henry Collins pull out from behind the big mansion. No doubt Jack Willard was taking his wife to town for the groceries, she decided. The car came along the road towards her at a fairly high speed. She kept to the left of the road, ready to wave as it passed. Then as it came close she felt a sudden fear. It wasn't going to pass! It was heading straight for her! With a scream she dropped the pail of berries and dodged toward the bushes. The car came careening after her!

# CHAPTER 6

SHE SCREAMED AGAIN as she hurled herself into the rough brush. The car's wheels seemed to thunder by within an inch of her; then it was gone. Whimpering, she raised herself from where she had fallen and stared numbly at the torn bushes. The car's tracks showed how deadly close it had been to her. For a moment she was completely unaware of anything but the fact she was still alive.

Then she vaguely realized that she heard excited voices. As things became clearer she could sort out a man's oaths and a woman crying and whining at the same time. She stepped out onto the road and saw that the car had come to a halt farther on, in the middle of the road, and Jack Willard and his wife were on their way back to her on foot.

Jack Willard was the first to reach her. He was perspiring and red faced, and looked like a giant stuffed toad in his tight dark uniform. He said, "Nothing I could do. The accelerator stuck and the car went out of control! I did my best not to hit you."

It had seemed to her he'd tried hard to do just the opposite. "I didn't realize what was happening until it was nearly too late," she said.

"You did the right thing," Jack growled uncomfortably. "I'll have to have her checked in the village. If I get to the village alive."

"Is it all right now?" Victoria asked dully.

He nodded. "Yes. Came free again just before I got her stopped.

But no telling how long it will stay that way."

Molly had joined them and, still uttering dry sobs, had listened to what they'd been saying. Now she spoke up. "Do you expect me to drive into town with you in that?"

"It'll be alright," he said, taking off his cap to mop his head with a soiled white handkerchief. The acrid odor of his perspiration hung about him. He glared at his shaken wife savagely. "We can do without your yowling!"

"I'm not going to risk my life in that car!" Molly Willard protested.

"I've told you once and I'll tell you again it's all right now!" her angry husband roared, looking as if he might hit her. To Victoria, who had been standing there without a word, he said, "You're not hurt?"

She might be wrong but it struck her there was disappointment in the tone of his question. She said, "No."

He replaced the cap on his head. "All right if I go on?"

"Yes."

Jack still hesitated. "I told you I was sorry. I hope you don't plan to make a big racket about it."

"Of course she will!" Molly interjected, her mood now turning to the anger of her husband. "Wouldn't you, if someone almost ran you down?"

Her husband drew himself up full height and stared straight ahead, seeming in danger of imminent apoplexy. Then he raised a threatening forefinger close to his wife's face. "It was an accident! Get that through your thick head! The accelerator stuck! I couldn't help it!"

"Please, go on," Victoria said, wanting to be rid of them. "I'm fine now. No need to hold you up any longer."

"Thanks a lot," the irate chauffeur said. Taking his wife by the arm roughly, he headed back in the direction of the car. "You see what I told you! But you know everything!" They argued all the way back to the car.

She still felt partly numbed as they got in the dark sedan and drove off. As they rounded a bend and vanished from sight she asked herself just how much faith she could put in Jack Willard's alibi. None, she decided.

To Victoria, it had seemed as if he'd deliberately tried to run her down. The story of the temporarily stuck accelerator that had so miraculously freed itself was just too pat. It was much more likely he'd intended to kill her and blame it on the car. Having failed, he'd fallen back on the alibi he would have offered in any case. And who could prove he wasn't telling the truth?

Why? That was the important question. Why had he made this attempt on her life? What was the motive and who was behind his action?

The sun had not come out from under the clouds again and the afternoon was dark and threatening. She had better get back to the safety of the house, she decided. She had scratched a hand in her fall but otherwise had come out of the accident unscathed. Now she slowly went back to the abandoned pail of strawberries and saw that although it was on its side only a few had spilled out. She bent over and retrieved the pail, scooping up the undamaged berries that lay beside it. Then she started back to Collins House.

Even the great mansion itself had a glowering aspect as she drew near it on this still, sullen afternoon. Thoroughly depressed, Victoria felt small and lost. She had reached out for love and understanding and thought she had found it at Collins House. She had been almost sure that Henry Collins was related to her and felt the secret of her identity would soon be revealed to her. Now she was again like a stranger in a cemetery she had happened to enter. She could walk among the orderly tombstones, read the inscriptions, search for familiar names and find none. Even if her father and mother were buried there, she wouldn't recognize their headstones.

When she entered the big dark kitchen Elizabeth turned from the washer and regarded her with surprise. "I didn't expect you back so soon," she said.

Victoria took note of the startled expression on the older woman's face. And for the first time she began to suspect Elizabeth. Elizabeth had sent her to the field; Elizabeth would know just about when she'd be starting back. Had she sent the car to run her down? Was the older woman aware of the friendship Henry Collins had shown her and the gift she had received? Did she fear the old man would cut off her and her daughter, Carolyn, in favor of Victoria? Could that be a motive for murder? Victoria thought not, at least in Elizabeth's case. Yet the mistress of the house was a strange, brooding woman who had not left its walls for close to twenty years. Surely not a normal person!

She put the pail of strawberries on the kitchen table and watching Elizabeth, said, "I almost had a bad accident."

The older woman's eyebrows raised. "Oh?"

"Yes. Coming back from the field. Jack Willard almost ran me down in your uncle's car."

Elizabeth looked shocked. "Was he drinking?"

"I couldn't tell. I was walking on the proper side of the road, close to the bushes. The car came directly at me. I saved myself by flinging myself in the brush."

"You're not hurt?"

"Just a scratch or two on my left hand."

"What was his excuse?"

"He claims the accelerator stuck and he lost control of the car."

A veiled look came into Elizabeth's eyes. "But you don't believe him?"

"I'd never be able to prove that wasn't what happened."

Elizabeth sighed and came over by the table. "I see," she said in an odd, distant voice. "You know how sorry I am. Yet there isn't much I can do beyond questioning this Jack Willard when he returns."

"I understand," Victoria said.

"Don't think I'll forget about it," Elizabeth said with new determination on her attractive face. "It is another of the things I'll want a satisfactory explanation for."

In spite of the older woman's show of sincerity, Victoria doubted that anything would be done. It was too difficult a situation. Jack Willard would be bound to protest his innocence.

The day remained humid and the sky gray and threatening. Once or twice Victoria heard the rumbling of distant thunder but no storm had developed in the area. Soon it was time for her to dress for the afternoon tea with Henry Collins. The way she felt now, she wasn't certain that she was going to enjoy it.

At a few minutes before four-thirty she met Elizabeth on the second landing. Victoria had put on a summer afternoon dress in a soft green shade and she saw that Elizabeth looked regally lovely in a long black satin skirt and a blouse of gold bead trim on a dark brown background, the collar raised a little at the back in a stiff flare. At her neck there hung a large cameo.

Elizabeth offered her a small smile. "I'm afraid I've dressed too formally. But I think Henry will forgive me. He likes things quite formal."

"You look very nice," Victoria assured her as they made their way along the long dark corridor to the rear wing of the mansion.

Benjamin was waiting for them at the door of the apartment. His gaunt face wore a smile. "Mr. Collins is expecting you in the large living-room," he said with a bow and led them through the closet entrance to the hidden room.

Because of the darkness of the afternoon, Henry Collins had turned on the ornate chandelier. It gave the crimson-walled room a soft, elegant glow. As Benjamin showed them in Henry rose from the chair before the fireplace and came across to greet them, leaning on the silver-headed cane.

"I've been looking forward to this," he said with a smile on his handsome, worn face. "Too bad it's such an unpleasant day. I'm sure we're due for a storm and soon."

"I'd say so too," Elizabeth agreed as they settled in the chairs that had been placed in a semicircle before the fireplace. "Still, your room is very cozy with the light on."

"I prefer it in here," the old man said. With a fleeting smile he added to Victoria, "I hop.e you don't find it stuffy and old hat, my dear."

"Not at all!" she assured him politely. She was seated between him and Elizabeth, almost directly facing the fireplace of white marble. The truth was that she still found the room oppressive and she was thinking of her near escape from death and wondering what the old man would say if he knew about it.

Benjamin wheeled in a tea table. Elizabeth poured while the old man passed out the cups and later offered plates of sandwiches and cake. In the pleasant, relaxed atmosphere conversation became more easy.

Elizabeth said over her teacup, "I hope Carolyn will soon be giving up her job in Bar Harbor and coming back home for a few weeks of rest before school begins again."

The old man smiled. "I hope so. I haven't seen her yet."

"I realize that," Elizabeth agreed. "I know she wouldn't want to miss you."

Victoria listened to this exchange with her mind far off. She had noticed Benjamin giving her odd looks as he'd helped serve the tea. Could he have discovered that she had the emeralds, despite Henry's precautions? Benjamin had been with Henry Collins so long he must be almost able to read his mind.

Thunder rumbled closer than it had before and for just a second the lights blinked out, leaving the big room filled with ominous shadows.

Henry Collins frowned. "The storm must be much nearer now."

"We often lose the lights for a while when we have a really bad one," Elizabeth admitted. And then with a more cheerful note, "Perhaps it will pass us by, after all."

The casual talk went on among them but the darkness that had so briefly cloaked the hidden room had apparently made them all a little uneasy. An eerie silence had come over the ancient mansion. Victoria felt it a prelude to the storm that was almost surely going to break soon.

"The car went to the village," Henry Collins said. "I hope they get back before the weather gets bad. I seem to remember flash rainstorms making the hill road from the village dangerous in the old days."

"It did wash away easily," Elizabeth agreed. "But we've spent a lot on improvements. I think it's quite safe now." As if she wanted to change the subject, she added, "We must have a really good wine for dinner tonight. To honor your dining with us."

The old man looked pleased. "The honor will be mine."

Remembering the unpleasant scene Roger had caused on the

last occasion when Henry Collins had joined them for dinner, Victoria couldn't help wondering what would happen this time. Her mind was set at ease by Elizabeth's next remark.

"Roger won't be with us tonight," she said. "He has to visit a friend in Bangor and won't be returning until late." Apparently she had known this and so had not hesitated to invite the old man to join them. "Do you have any preference in wine, Uncle Henry?"

He shook his head. "I leave it entirely up to you."

Elizabeth smiled. "In that case I'll select champagne. We have some very good stock left in the cellar." She glanced Victoria's way. "I'll give you the key to the wine cellar and the number of the bottle and let you bring up one for us when we leave here."

"Champagne was the great drink of my youth," the old man said. "I suppose more champagne flowed at the Ritz Hampton than in any hotel in New York. This very room we sit in now almost always had an iced bottle or two of champagne in it awaiting the casual visitor."

"You must tell Victoria more about what it was like then," the older woman suggested. "You remember the stories you used to tell me about Ziegfeld and his shows and the lovely showgirls who were your friends."

He shook his head. "That seems another world today. I doubt if anything Broadway offers now equals the lavish, extravagant splendor of Ziegfeld at his best."

There was a definite note of sadness in his voice. It was plain he must also be recalling some great tragedy along with the good memories. For Henry Collins there would always be this ghost from the past to haunt him. She recalled his mention of the girl he had loved and the thin, sweet sound of the voice on the ancient record—all that was left alive of his long lost romance.

Staring at the crimson wallpaper and the gold-framed prints of that other day, she found herself deep in the atmosphere of the hidden room. She lost track of the conversation of the other two as she tried to think what it had been like and guess what had happened here to change Henry Collins from a jovial dandy to a bitter recluse. And for no reason she could understand the shadowy vision of that girl in the wide-brimmed hat and veil crossed her mind—the girl whose phantom figure she'd felt sure she'd seen in her room. Elizabeth had blamed it on a curtain moving in the wind, but couldn't she have been mistaken? It had been real enough to convince her. And as this thought troubled her, the bulbs in the ancient chandelier dimmed alarmingly once more and stayed dim without actually going out.

The old man's voice broke into her reverie as he said, "There were so many beauties in the Ziegfeld shows, Dolores, Jessica Reed, Vera Maxwell, Lillian Lorraine and Kay Laurell."

"And you knew most of them," Elizabeth said, her outline blurred in the dim light.

"They were all my friends," Henry agreed.

Victoria didn't recognize any of the names. She thought how lonely it must be for the old man to go on living so many years with only his remembrance of this long-ago world to sustain him.

The thunder rumbled more loudly now and seemed very close. Victoria glanced at the space of window between the heavy crimson drapes in time to see the sharp flash of lightning. And now the rain came with a startling abruptness. It all combined to make the deeply-shadowed room seem weird. She turned her attention to the barely glowing light bulbs of the chandelier. It seemed likely they would fade out completely at any moment.

Elizabeth spoke in a hushed voice, "We're going to get the storm."

Henry Collins had sunk deep in the wing chair and did not seem to have heard her. He was staring straight ahead with glazed eyes. "And there was Olive Thomas," he said in his dry voice. "The loveliest of them all. I'll never forget the night I heard of her suicide."

Victoria's attention was caught by this reference to suicide. She was sure it was closely related in the old man's mind to the happenings long ago in this room. Had the great love of his life committed suicide as well? And here?

Victoria said, "I don't think I ever heard of her."

As if on cue the lights went out completely and left them all sitting there in near darkness. Only when the occasional shaft of lightning pierced the shadows with a blue gleam was there any break in the gloom. The rain continued to pour down and the thunder now made the room quiver with its threat.

"Of course, Olive Thomas!" Elizabeth said in the darkness. "She did kill herself. I'd forgotten!"

"It is easy for some to forget." Henry Collins spoke above the sound of the rain. "I can never forget," he said. "That Halloween night. That last meeting. Such things you never forget."

Victoria leaned forward in her chair, her heart pounding. He had come back to the mystery of the room now and she felt sure he might be ready to reveal it. He was talking to himself as he sat there in the shadows.

"It had come to an end," the old man said, just a voice emerging from the darkness now. "I never saw her again."

"You mustn't hark back to it so!" Elizabeth remonstrated with him.

"What else would you have me do?" There was bitterness and anger in his voice. "As long as this room exists she remains real! Nearby! I know it!"

Victoria knew the chilling fear she'd experienced so many times before in the hidden room. It surged through her as she listened to the old man's words. Henry Collins was convinced the dead girl's spirit was bound to this old room. And perhaps it was!

The thunder boomed so close it rattled the window after a lightning flash sharper than any before. She caught a brief glimpse of the old man's pale, troubled face in its flash. And then a door creaked open and the spectral form of Benjamin glided into the room with a tall candlestick and candle in his hand.

"I knew you would be needing this," he said in his harsh voice as he placed it on the table. "The lights seem to have gone off for good."

Elizabeth's lovely profile showed against the flickering candle light. "Thank you," she told him. "Probably a transformer has been blown out and we may not have lights or power for some time."

Henry Collins sat forward in his chair, seeming to have recovered from his wandering. "It's too bad," he said. "It has spoiled our little party."

"Not at all," Elizabeth said.

Victoria managed a smile for the old man. "It has been very interesting," she said.

Elizabeth stood up. "Now we must leave if I'm to have dinner prepared on time for you." Victoria got up as well.

Henry Collins saw them to the door. "Would you prefer to cancel our dinner plans?" he suggested. "I can come down another night."

"No. Let's go ahead as we'd decided," Elizabeth insisted. "The lights may come on. And if they don't, we have plenty of candles."

Benjamin was waiting for them just outside the door with another candle in his hand. He bowed. "I'll see you safely back to the main house, ladies." And he led them along the dark corridor.

Victoria was caught up in the strange mood the violent thunderstorm had brought to the old mansion. In the flickering light of the single candle, it almost seemed as if they'd been transported to another age.

Watching Benjamin walk solemnly along, she was struck by the way he held his shoulders and head. There was no hint of the stooped weakness so evident in Henry Collins. Yet the two men must be almost the same age. And for half a century they had lived in close proximity and known each other's thoughts and deeds. Benjamin Willard must know all the details of the tragedy of the hidden room, although there was no likelihood of his ever revealing his master's secret.

She frowned as she followed the old man and Elizabeth in the near darkness. What had Henry Collins' gift of emeralds to do with it? Where did they fit in the tragedy? Had they belonged to the dead girl? Or had the old man acquired them someplace else, years later? He seemed to have lingered over the suicide of Olive Thomas. It struck her that this other girl might also have taken her life.

When they reached the lower hallway Benjamin left them, after giving them the candle and insisting that they would need it. He made his way up the stairs to vanish in the darkness. They went on to the kitchen where Elizabeth discovered an oil lamp in one of the cupboards and lit it and placed it on the table. The thunder and lightning had passed, but the downpour of rain continued and it was weirdly dark for the time of day.

"That's more cheerful," Elizabeth said with a smile. "Now I'll get on with dinner. I can prepare it on the wood range and perhaps before everything in the refrigerator spoils, the lights will come back on."

Victoria asked, "What can I do to help?"

"There's the wine," the older woman said. "The shelf is marked eleven. Take any bottle on that shelf that's handy. I'll get you the key."

Taking a candle, Victoria made her way to the cellar door and went down the steep wooden stairway, its steps worn in deep hollows from the passage up and down them for close to two hundred years! It made little difference on this expedition whether the lights were on or not, since the lighting in the cellar area was very poor anyway and the wiring did not extend to the older portion of it which had been shut off for some time.

The wine cellar was near this closed area, but still part of the more modern section. A wave of damp, musty air assailed her nostrils as she reached the bottom of the stairs. It took her a moment to decide which way she should turn. In absolute darkness the cellar did appear slightly different. The flickering of the candle as she moved along cast weird shadows on the stone walls of the deep cellar.

She had heard Roger and Elizabeth once discussing the possibility of an even lower cellar at a level beneath this one. It had been mentioned in some notes belonging to their grandfather, but neither of them had ever been able to locate an entrance to it. They had decided it must have been sealed up years before, as not necessary. This often happened to areas of these very old buildings. She knew that many rooms upstairs had been closed off to the ravages of dust, cobwebs and dampness.

Victoria halted a moment as she came to another turning and debated which way she would proceed from there. This time she decided it was the passage to the right. She seemed to have gone a tremendous distance. She noticed the dampness on the stone walls here as contrasted to the dry surface of the other passage. Her footsteps echoed as she continued her journey to the wine cellar. In the muted silence down there, the sound of the storm had been left behind.

She knew she was reaching the end of the passage and was near the door to the wine cellar now. And then just ahead she saw it. Approaching the familiar plank door with its heavy padlock, she managed the candle in one hand while she unlocked it with the key Elizabeth had given her. Swinging the heavy door open, she went through the low entrance into the wine cellar itself.

Here the ceiling was just an inch or so above her head. The pungent odor of hogsheads that had held their rich cargo of wines and ales in years gone by still gave the section a character of its own. The casks, long since empty, were stacked around the walls at various points and dusty racks in the center still held a good selection of wine. She held the candle high to seek out the numbers on the various shelves. It took her a moment to discover that eleven was on the second rack. There she saw at least seven or eight dust-covered bottles protruding and took one down.

Her task completed, she left the wine cellar and locked it again. She was beginning to retrace her steps along the damp stone passage when from directly ahead there came a sound that froze her in her tracks and curdled her blood.

A soft female voice mournfully called her name. "Victoria! Victoria!" It rose and fell in a fantastic manner as the soft voice echoed along the stone passages.

She stood there, too terrified to move. Certainly it hadn't been Elizabeth's voice. This was an eerie, unearthly cry like the lament of a dying creature.

The candle was burning dangerously low and now it fluttered as a draught caught it. Victoria gave it a frightened glance. She knew she couldn't face being left here in the dark. Thinking she must have imagined the call, she began to hurry forward once more.

Again she was halted by the mournful, "Victoria! Victoria!"

Trembling, she leaned against the damp wall and stared fearfully ahead in the direction from which the cries had come. "Who is it? What do you want?" she cried.

There was no reply, just her own echo. She really hadn't expected much more, she thought, as she crouched against the damp stones of the cellar wall. What to do now?

Then the full force of her panic hit her. For in the murky passage ahead she saw the blurred figure of the girl in the wide hat and veil gradually take form. She watched with the fascination of pure horror as the figure pressed nearer and she could make out the flowing skirt, the narrow waist, even a fur around the girl's shoulders.

It was too much! With a strangled scream she dropped the candle and bottle of champagne and turned to race down the corridor from which she'd just come. Sobbing and panting, not knowing where she was heading, she fled the phantom, hoping that somehow she would find a stairway to escape the cursed depths. In her haste and confusion she bumped into a wall with such force that it nearly stunned her.

As she paused, she heard the voice cry her name again close behind, "Victoria!" The wailing was only a short distance away.

"No!" she screamed. Again she turned in the cavernous darkness and ran on. It was simple madness now. She was racing on without any idea of where she was. And then she came to a solid wall. Again the impact of coming upon it so suddenly left her gasping and leaning weakly against it. Her knuckles hurt from abrasions and she was nauseated with fear. Groping along the side of the wall, she tried to find a passage of escape. But it was all solid wall, no matter which way she turned. She had come to a dead end.

Now she could only wait and hope the horror she had witnessed so vividly would not catch up with her. She was trapped there in the musty darkness.

The sound of her own breathing seemed to drown out everything else as she waited there. Eyes widened by terror, she strained to see some shadow take shape in the blackness. And then she was certain she heard a rustling from a few feet away.

The voice was a whisper close by. "Victoria!"

# CHAPTER 7

VICTORIA FELT she had come to the end of her endurance. There was no longer any fight left in her. Closing her eyes, she waited for whatever fate had in store. A moment passed and then another and nothing had happened. And now she opened her eyes again and to her surprise she was no longer in darkness. From the end of the stone-walled passage she could see a dim light!

It could only mean one thing. The electricity had come on again and someone had switched on the cellar lights. Probably Elizabeth had decided to come down and do this as soon as the power returned. Her fears subsiding, she went forward quickly and found this short side passage joined to the main cellar corridor. Taking it for a short distance, she reached another junction of passages and coming toward her along the one to her left was Elizabeth.

Victoria went to meet her. "I thought you must have come down when I saw the lights on."

The older woman stared at her. "I wondered what was keeping you. And when the lights returned I thought I'd better come down and turn them on. I was afraid you might have fallen and hurt yourself or lost your way." She paused. "You do look as if you'd been through an ordeal."

"I'd call it that."

"What happened?"

"Nothing, until I had the wine and was on my way back," Victoria said. "Then I heard someone calling my name in a ghostly voice. And the same figure I saw in my room that night emerged from the shadows."

Elizabeth looked skeptical but she said, "Go on."

"I'm afraid I lost my courage. I called out and received no reply. Then I turned and ran. I dropped both the candle and the wine. I kept on running in the darkness and the voice seemed to follow me. It was terrifying!"

The other woman sighed. "I shouldn't have sent you down here alone with the lights out."

"You couldn't know what was going to happen."

Elizabeth seemed more resigned than sympathetic. "I know you are nervous of the dark. It doesn't take a lot to make you see ghosts!"

Victoria's cheeks burned. "I didn't imagine any of this. I'm sure something awful would have happened if you hadn't turned the lights on. I don't say it was a ghost, but I do believe it was someone pretending to be one. Someone who meant me harm!" And for just a moment she wondered whether it could have been Elizabeth herself.

"Why should anyone pretend to be a ghost?" Elizabeth asked sharply.

Victoria was on the point of mentioning the emeralds but stopped herself. "I don't know," she said in a small voice.

"Nor do I," the older woman said. "I noticed the broken wine bottle you dropped back there. We'll have to go and get another bottle of champagne. I assume you haven't lost the key?"

"No. I have it here." She gave it to Elizabeth.

"We may as well go back now and get it over with, in case the power should fail again."

The power didn't go off and the storm passed as quickly as it had come. By the time Victoria went upstairs again it was much brighter. The incident in the cellar had a nightmare quality that made it seem highly improbable. And she was convinced that the ghostly figure had been someone trying to terrify her.


From the kitchen where she helped Elizabeth prepare dinner, she saw that Henry Collins' car was back again. This meant both Jack Willard and his wife, Molly, were somewhere in the house. Recalling the moment when she had almost been run down on her way back from the strawberry field, she realized that twice within the last few hours there had been deliberate attacks on her. It was only good luck that had saved her in each instance. And the trouble had begun with Henry Collins confiding in her and making her the gift of the emeralds. Yet he hadn't told her enough.

She kept thinking of this all through dinner—a dinner that went very well. The vintage champagne was delicious and Henry Collins became quite relaxed and good company. He rambled at length over the famous hotels and eating places in New York during his heyday, and for a time it seemed he had put aside his tragic memories to linger over the happy ones.

After dinner they went into the big living room and Elizabeth provided the old man with a cigar and a glass of brandy. He had barely seated himself when the front doorbell rang. It turned out to be one of the officials from the packing company with a problem that demanded Elizabeth's attention as a director. She excused herself and led the newcomer to the study, leaving Henry Collins and Victoria alone.

She was standing by the fireplace in the big room. He got up to come forward and study the large oil portrait of the first Collins to settle in Collinsport, Jeremiah Collins. He gave the portrait a close inspection and turned to her with a smile.

"When I was very young my mother used to scare me into good behavior by warning me old Jeremiah would come after me if I wasn't good," he said. "I've always felt he had an evil face, ever since."

"Put it down to childish fancies," she agreed.

He leaned on his silver-headed cane as he stood facing her. "I suppose so." He gave the portrait of the rather forbidding, hook-nosed ancestor another glance. "But you must admit he doesn't look to be the kindest person who ever lived."

"He has a strong face."

"A cruel face," Henry Collins corrected her, and eyed the portrait once more. "Look at those tight, thin lips, the firm set of the jaw and those eyes. They have a wicked gleam."

"Perhaps the painter gave him qualities he didn't have in life."

"I doubt it," the old man said, turning to her again. "If you know the family history you will have read some strange things about Jeremiah."

"I'm afraid I'm not too well versed in the Collins history," she confessed.

"Nor any reason why you should be," the old man said. He moved back to the chair and settled down in it with a sigh. Then he picked up his glass of brandy and took a sip. "You know Jeremiah was a sea captain, I suppose."

"Yes."

"New England sailing ships were famous all around the world in those days," Henry went on, his eyes on the portrait again. "There were great profits to be made. Men could become wealthy in a lifetime. Found a dynasty that would survive them for generations. Old Jeremiah accomplished all that."

She smiled. "Then I suppose he had to be ruthless and determined to achieve such a goal."

"Yes," he agreed. "He couldn't let minor qualms upset him. As I said, there were great profits to be made. Especially if the shipowners weren't too fussy about the sort of cargo they dealt in."

She frowned. "You mean?"

"I'm sure you know what I mean. I'm referring to Black Gold!"

"Black Gold?" she repeated blankly.

The old man appeared to be enjoying himself. "That's what they called it. A polite name for the slave trade. Old Jeremiah was mixed up in his share of slaving. And from that wicked foundation came the Collins fortune."

Victoria looked at the portrait again and was ready to agree Jeremiah Collins did have a cruel countenance. She said, "I'd never heard that before."

"The family isn't exactly proud of the story," Henry Collins conceded with a wry expression on his lined face. "And some people say that's why Collins House has seen so much tragedy. They claim our family bears a curse. A curse dating back to Africa a hundred and fifty years ago."

She looked at him. "Surely you don't think that?"

His face took on a strange expression. "Perhaps I do."

"But that's a horrible thought!" she protested.

"Consider the record," he said calmly. "Our family seems to have had more than its fair share of suicides, murders, and unhappy marriages. Not to mention the accidents and the bad blood that exists between some branches of the family."

She said, "In other words, you're interpreting events through superstition."

The old man smiled sadly. "If Jeremiah Collins was in the slave trade as the records indicate, you can be certain he murdered more than one man in the course of his career. Not that it would be called murder. They'd probably put it down to an unfortunate loss of salable goods."

Victoria shivered. "I don't think you should speak of murder so lightly."

His eyes met hers. "The mark of Cain," he said. "It revolts you the same as it does most people. And yet the majority of murderers are not the fiends we imagine but people remarkably like ourselves, save in one respect."

"I find that hard to believe."

"Possibly," he said. "You are still very young. You haven't

experienced life as I have. A reckless action, a fit of temper, an error in judgment, any of these could easily make a killer of the most temperate of individuals. The courts prove that every day."

She studied him with puzzled eyes. "You sound as if you were arguing in favor of murderers."

"I'm only trying to point out that while Jeremiah Collins might have killed in an accidental way, he was not necessarily guilty of premeditated murder nor a black-dyed villain."

"I find it hard to draw a line about murder," she said, glancing again at the portrait. "And I must say there seems little about Jeremiah Collins to admire, aside from his perseverance."

The old man took the last sip of his brandy. "At least you bow to that," he said.

She looked toward the doorway of the living room to make sure no one was coming and then she took a few steps to bring her close to the old man. And in a low voice, she confided, "Since the other afternoon, my life has been threatened."

A shadow crossed Henry Collins' face. Leaning on the silver-headed cane, he raised himself to his feet with difficulty. "We shouldn't talk about it here," he warned her. "Tell me later."

She lowered her voice to a desperate whisper. "But I may not get a chance. Benjamin always seems to be around and he tries to stop us talking."

The old man nodded. "I understand."

"Today his son tried to run me down in the car."

"No!"

"Yes!" she insisted. "Elizabeth has promised to look into it, but I know she probably won't do anything. And someone frightened me in the cellar this afternoon and I'm sure if Elizabeth hadn't come, would have tried to harm me."

The old man stared at her in alarm. "Who?"

"I don't know," she said. "I think it must have to do with" — she hesitated—"your gift."

He quickly raised a forefinger to his lips in a frantic gesture for silence. "Leave it in my hands," he begged. "I'll speak to Jack Willard and hear what he has to say. He probably was drinking."

"He's nearly always drinking," Victoria said with disgust. "But I don't call that any excuse."

"Benjamin will talk to him. I'll demand that he offer a sound explanation or I'll discharge him," the old man promised.

Victoria listened without any special hope. She expected Jack Willard would say there had been no real danger to her and his wife would undoubtedly back him up. It would be two to one against her and Henry Collins would wind up thinking she was a victim of her imagination as the others seemed to.

The discussion was brought to an end as Elizabeth appeared with her caller and saw him to the door. When she had said goodnight to him, she came back to the living room and joined Victoria and Henry Collins once again. From that point on the conversation followed routine channels and the old man soon excused himself and went upstairs.

And so the rather hectic day ended with a quiet evening. Victoria was alarmed by the attacks she had endured and startled at finding the Collins family history bore some black marks. She was beginning to understand why Burke Devlin had warned her she might be happier outside the fold than a member of it. Once again she realized how dependent on him she had become for good advice and how often he had willingly given it. She made up her mind to see him again at the first opportunity. The gossips of Collinsport might talk, but she was willing to run the risk. Burke was the best substitute at hand for the distant Ernest Collins. She fell asleep thinking about the young violinist with whom she had fallen in love.

The next morning was bright and warm with no hint of the storm clouds and humidity of the previous day. It was perfect Maine weather. She hurried to finish her household tasks with the idea of going down to the beach for a while. She was in the lower hallway when a sober-faced Benjamin came down the stairs.

"I'm glad to find you here, miss," he said. "I have something to tell you."

Facing him, she said, "Yes?"

He sighed deeply. "This is most awkward for me, miss. But Mr. Henry asked me to speak to you about the matter."

"It's all right, Benjamin," she said quietly. "I believe I know what you're hinting at."

"I understand you had a very close call yesterday."

"That is true."

"You discussed the accident with Mr. Collins."

"Yes, I did."

"And that you claim my son was to blame."

"He was at the wheel of the car."

The old servant's face was a mask of concern. He glanced around nervously and then leaned forward to her. "I must confess Jack is a very wild boy," he said in a troubled voice.

The idea of the brazen, stout, middle-aged man being referred to as a boy had its comic side which she wasn't able to appreciate at that moment. She said, "I'm not in a position to make a comment on his character. But I do know he nearly ran me down and I'm not satisfied with the excuse he offered."

Benjamin nodded gravely. "He was drinking, miss. I know that. I smelled the liquor on his breath as he came down the stairs that morning. We had a quarrel about it."

She recalled hearing them argue on the steps although she had not known what it was about. She said, "His wife was with him. She should be able to tell what happened."

"Molly is a very weak woman," the old man said scornfully. "Not to be counted on at all. I dare say she'd say anything Jack told her to."

Victoria gave him a bleak look. "And they'll both deny any negligence on their part."

"Very likely," he admitted with a sigh. "But I have told Mr. Henry, and I'm telling you, that Jack understands there must be no more mistakes. If he steps out of line once more I'll not have him around."

"I hope he understands that you mean it."

"I do mean it," Benjamin said grimly. "Count on that, miss."

"I suppose it will have to satisfy me," she said. "I don't blame you, of course."

"Thank you, miss," the old servant said. "I think highly of you and so does Mr. Henry. I'm sure he's let you know that?"

Victoria was suddenly on the alert. The old man had put the question to her in such a casual way. It had been worked into their talk innocently and yet she had the feeling he was probing again—trying to find out what Henry Collins had confided in her.

She said, "You know as much about that as I do."

Benjamin smiled coldly. "Not quite, miss. There are a few things Mr. Henry does not tell me. If you will recall, he insisted I leave you alone with him the other day."

"Yes, I do remember," she said.

"He has an unusual interest in you, miss." Benjamin's eyes bored into her.

Suddenly she felt confused and groped to find something to say. "Perhaps it is because I remind him of someone," she suggested.

"Yes," the old man nodded. "Yes. I do believe that is it. Mr. Collins is given to strange impulses at times. One can never be sure what he will do next."

"Oh?"

"Indeed it is true, miss," Benjamin continued, his eyes still fixed on her. "Take this morning, for instance. He has decided he wants to take a drive around the countryside in the car. Most unusual. Normally he dislikes leaving the house. But he has built up some sentimental interest in seeing some of the old landmarks again. So I'm on my way now to tell Jack to bring the car around."

"It is a lovely day," Victoria said. "I can understand that he might suddenly have a yearning to see some of the familiar places in the area."

"That's the way it is with him, miss," the old man said. "But then it is easy to forgive him, since his time can certainly not be long." And with a nod he went on out the front door, leaving her alone.

She went on to the kitchen to help Elizabeth with the work there. A short time later she heard the car come around to the front. Benjamin returned upstairs to bring Henry Collins down and they drove off on their sightseeing trip.

Elizabeth, busy polishing some of the elaborate silverware which had been in the family for generations, looked up from her work on a massive teapot with a smile and said, "So Uncle Henry has decided to take a drive at last. I think that's wonderful."

She nodded agreement. "It should do him good to get out."

"And you should be getting yourself some fresh air as well," Elizabeth said with a sudden look of concern. "You are feeling alright after yesterday?"

"Yes. Benjamin apologized to me just now for his son's driving."

"I spoke to him," Elizabeth told her. "And I let him understand I wanted a full explanation."

"Mr. Collins mentioned it to him," Victoria said. "He promised nothing like it would happen again."

"I should hope not!" Elizabeth said indignantly. She put the huge shining teapot aside to pick up a small pitcher that was badly tarnished and begin polishing it.

Victoria spoke now to get the older woman's reaction. "In a way, I was more upset by what happened in the cellar."

Elizabeth paused in her work to stare at her with an almost guilty expression on her attractive face. "I'd nearly forgotten about that."

"Someone did come after me and cry out my name in a weird way."

The older woman frowned. "You seem so sure. Yet I saw no one when I went down there."

Victoria decided if the older woman was pretending she was giving an excellent performance. She still suspected that it might have been Elizabeth herself who had played the role of phantom, although she was not certain why. And if not Elizabeth, it could have been Molly Willard.

"There was someone or something down there," Victoria asserted.

Elizabeth raised an eyebrow. "You make it sound as if you suspect a ghost again?"

"I think that is what I'm meant to believe," Victoria said with a touch of bitterness. "Someone is working very hard to make me believe it."

The older woman sighed with displeasure. "I do wish you'd stop brooding about it and go enjoy this lovely summer day."

Victoria accepted her words as a dismissal. And she was glad of the chance to go to the beach. With Henry Collins and his retinue away the old house seemed strangely silent. She went upstairs to her room and changed into her bathing suit; then she put on a robe over it and started for the beach. She took the path along the cliff and when she reached the high point where the bench was, she paused a moment.

She was sitting there gazing out across the sparkling silver ocean when a shadow fell across her. She glanced up with alarm on her intelligent, attractive face. The source of the shadow was a tall, balding man dressed in somber black and standing directly behind her, his hat in hand.

He smiled and when he spoke it was in a hollow, sepulchral tone. "I fear I've frightened you!"

Victoria stood up and stared at him. His sober dark suit and tie together with his starched white shirt gave him the look of an undertaker. Besides being tall he was gaunt. His pale face with its hawk nose and piercing eyes gave him a predatory air. The thin lips stayed parted to reveal oversize white teeth in a mocking smile.

She said, "I didn't hear you come up."

The eyes appraised her boldly. "I'm sorry. I didn't intentionally make a stealthy approach. You must forgive me."

"It's all right," she said, suddenly aware that he was staring at her intently and realizing the thin robe gave her small protection over her bathing suit. She resented his brazen study of her and wondered who he was.

As if reading her thoughts, he said, "You are undoubtedly wondering who I am?" He spoke in that strange but impressive hollow manner again.

She tried to calm her mounting fears that he was insane, glancing toward the distant Collins House and vainly looking for some sign of activity there. But there was none. However, she did see a strange car in the driveway before the house, a dark sedan.

Swallowing hard, she said, "Is that your car?"

The tall, hawk-faced man continued to smile. "Yes, it is. I suppose I should have gone directly to the house and announced by arrival. But I saw you walking along here and assuming you were one of the Collins family, I decided to make myself known to you first."

"I see," she said, although she was still confused. "I'm Victoria Winters. I work here. I was on my way to the beach."

"Victoria Winters!" the man said with the air of one making a great discovery. "Of course! Roger told me all about you!"

"You're a friend of Roger's, then?"

"Yes." The man nodded. "Roger invited me down here for a few days. I've been in Augusta on business. My name is Rupert Harvey and I happen to be a psychometrist."

"I think I've heard Mr. Collins mention you," she said. "But he didn't say anything about your coming for a visit."

"I wasn't sure I could make it until this morning." He looked back toward Collins House. "But Roger told me so many fascinating stories about this place I didn't want to leave the area without giving it a few days." He turned to her again. "I assume you know what a psychometrist is?"

"I'm afraid I don't."

He laughed easily. "That's quite understandable. Mine is not a well-known profession. I have a natural sensitivity to objects and places. By merely touching things I can often infer many facts from them. I have been in continual demand by various law enforcement groups. That was why I came to Augusta."

"It sounds interesting," she said. "And a little frightening, as well."

Rupert Harvey regarded her indulgently. "You needn't be afraid of me, Miss Winters. I try to use my peculiar talents with discretion. But from what Roger told me about Collins House there must be a great deal to interest me here."

"It is an old house."

Harvey nodded. "From what he has said, a house of shadowed secrets and many sorrows. I'm sure I can learn a great deal here."

"Mr. Collins has gone to his office at the plant," she said. "But I can phone him when we return to the house. I'm sure he'll be glad to know you've arrived."

The tall man raised a protesting hand. "Please don't let me take you back to the house," he said. "I can find my way alone and introduce myself to Mrs. Stoddard." He offered that peculiar knowing smile again. "I understand she is always at home."

Victoria found her dislike for the thin man increasing. She wondered how much Roger had revealed about the family's secrets. It was apparent he'd discussed her and gone into his sister's problem and the fact she had never set foot outside Collins House in nearly twenty years. If Rupert Harvey had tried to drain him of information when he was drinking, no doubt the tall man had found out a lot more.

She said, "I don't mind going back with you. Mrs. Stoddard often takes a short nap at this time of day and it mightn't be convenient for her to let you in." As she said this she took a step toward him.

He seemed pleased by her words. "Extremely kind of you." And then glancing about him and giving an especially close look at the bench, he told her, "I sense a feeling of strife in this spot." He reached forward and touched long, white fingers to the back of the bench, a severe expression crossing his gaunt features as he did so. He concentrated for a moment.

Then he turned to her with a frown. "I sense violence here," he said. "I can feel it. Violence and despair."

The firm note of conviction in his voice astonished her. She studied the bizarre dark-garbed figure standing there with his slender hand resting on the green wooden bench and in spite of the bright warm sun a sudden chill went through her. She said, "You must be remarkably sensitive. There has been at least one suicide from this cliff." Even as she spoke, she realized that Roger might have already told the psychometrist this fact and he had used his knowledge in a tricky way to impress her.

"More than one," he almost intoned, frowning in his concentration. "This is not a happy spot, despite the magnificent view." And he removed his hand from the bench.

"I'd almost forgotten about it until you reminded me just now."

"I'm sorry," he said. "I have no desire to spoil these pleasant surroundings for you."

She glanced down at the rocky beach below and gave a small shiver as the waves rushed in with an angry surge. "You haven't really," she said. "I'm familiar with all that has happened here." She began to stroll back toward the house with him.

He donned his soft black hat, which seemed heavy for the summer season. He matched his stride to hers and seemed amiable enough as they made their way along the path. "Roger told me you have some interesting visitors," he said. "His uncle."

"Yes."

Harvey paused significantly. "I believe there is a room. A particularly interesting room, to which the old man is greatly attached."

She nodded. "Yes." Obviously there wasn't much that Roger hadn't told this weird stranger.

When they reached the house it was just as she'd predicted. Elizabeth had gone upstairs for her usual brief noontime nap. Victoria showed the stranger into the living room and went to the study to phone Roger Collins at his office. It took some minutes to locate Roger.

His voice came over the line in an irritable fashion. "What's the trouble?" he wanted to know.

"There's a Rupert Harvey here," she explained. "He says you

invited him to visit for a few days."

"Rupert Harvey!" Roger repeated the name as if he'd never heard it. And then he groaned. "Now I remember! Fellow I met in the hotel bar in Augusta. I believe I did mention his coming down. Never thought he'd accept! You say he's there now?"

"Yes," she said. "Elizabeth is resting. Shall I show him to a guest room?"

"Naturally," Roger said indignantly. "May turn out to be useful. Claims to be a psychometrist. Give him the room next to mine on the second floor. I'll get home in an hour or so. You can tell him."

Victoria promised she would and hung up, feeling uneasy about the whole business. She was not sure how Elizabeth would react—and she had missed her chance to go to the beach. On top of it all she felt Rupert Harvey was a truly strange individual and was not sure what problems his coming might bring to the already troubled house. She hurried along the hallway to the shadowed living room where she had left him seated in a wing chair. When she got there she stood for a moment with an expression of growing surprise. Harvey was no longer there. He had vanished completely!

# CHAPTER 8

VICTORIA STOOD THERE in surprise for a moment, then glanced toward the stairs. Rupert Harvey might have decided to make an exploration of the old house on his own. She didn't doubt that Roger had given him at least a rough description of the floor-plan of the old mansion, along with all the other details.

With mixed feelings of anger and fear she hurried to the stairway and quickly made her way up to the second floor. At once she headed down along the dark corridor that led to the rear of the house and the wing in which the hidden room was located. When she arrived at the entrance to the elaborate crimson and white room it was no surprise to find Rupert Harvey standing there in the doorway.

He turned to her with that nasty mocking smile. "I suppose you wondered where I had gone."

In a tone of reproach, she said, "I did miss you."

"Actually, I should apologize for taking the liberty of coming up here," he said, the piercing eyes meeting hers with a cold look. "But Roger described the place so well I knew I'd have no difficulty finding it."

"Mr. Henry Collins, who occupies this section of the house, is out at the moment," she said, knowing she sounded prim and vexed. "It might upset him to come back and find us here."

Rupert Harvey turned to eye the room again and took a step

into it. "But this fascinates me more than anything else about Collins House," he protested.

"I'm sure Mr. Henry Collins will be happy to invite you here in good time," she said. "But it would be wiser to wait until you are invited. He's rather peculiar on this subject."

Rupert Harvey glanced at her with that annoying smile again. "So I understand."

Her dislike for the tall, formidable man was growing every minute. "I reached Roger on the phone. He promised he would be back here shortly."

"Excellent," Rupert Harvey said in an abstracted voice, still carefully studying the room and its contents. "What a remarkable place this is."

"Your room is to be on the second floor, but in the main wing and next to Roger's. If you'll come with me now, I'll show it to you."

"Thank you," he said without enthusiasm. Ignoring her obvious desire to leave the room he nonchalantly went forward to examine the magazine and newspaper on the table.

"I really do think we should leave," she said. "Mr. Henry Collins could be returning at any moment and I don't think he should find us here."

Harvey raised a slender hand to her in a gesture that begged for silence. He was frowning and standing there with a strangely intent look. "Please!" he said in a low voice.

Her eyes widened at his unusual behavior. His hand was resting on the magazine that lay on the table, the fifty-year-old magazine with its cover reproduction of a Gibson girl drawing. And she was convinced that his sensitive fingers were delivering some sort of message about the room. A message that would have to do with its unhappy history. And suddenly she began to feel that Roger had encouraged him to come to Collins House for this purpose. To delve into the tragic legend of the room and expose Henry Collins and his part in it.

She asked, "What is it?"

"This room has known horror," was his tense answer. He stared ahead as if listening to sounds she could not hear.

Victoria was startled by his statement, the more so since she had the same unhappy feeling about the old room. She said, "You sound very sure of this."

"I am," he said, turning to her with his face clouded with annoyance. "Had I the time and the proper conditions I could concentrate further and perhaps come up with some real facts concerning the tragedy this room has known."

"You mean a sort of séance?"

He shrugged his broad shoulders. "I suppose you could call it that. My work is divided into three categories: telepathy, clairvoyance and precognition. This is a situation where my clairvoyant powers would be chiefly brought into play." Again she was struck by the sinister note about him.

With a small shiver she said, "I have never believed in such things."

His eyes were malevolent as he said, "You are very young, Miss Winters. You have a lot to learn in life."

"Yes. I suppose that is true." Her answer was hushed.

Now he gave her tense nerves a measure of relief by turning and starting out of the hidden room. He joined her in the doorway and paused to give it a final glance. "I will make it a point to come back," he said. "And then we will know more."

Victoria made no reply to this, but led him back along the hallway to the main wing and his own room. After she left him there she went directly to Elizabeth's room and tapped gently on the door. An invitation to enter reached her in the older woman's familiar voice. She went inside and found Elizabeth seated in a chair by the window overlooking the ocean. Quickly she told her the story.

Elizabeth at once got up with a sigh. "I do wish Roger would give us more warning when he expects guests," she said. "But then, that would be expecting too much of him!"

"This Rupert Harvey is very strange," Victoria said.

The older woman gave her a look of amused irony. "From what he has said and done, I'd surely be willing to agree."

Her plan to go swimming abandoned, Victoria went on up to her room and changed back into clothes suitable for the warm summer afternoon. While she was still up there she saw Henry Collins' limousine come into the drive and stop before the front door. After a moment the old man was assisted from the car by Benjamin and his son. Seeing how feeble he appeared, even with the support of the other two, she guessed that the drive had been too tiring for him and he was now on the point of collapse. A conversation on the second landing with Benjamin a little while afterward confirmed her supposition.

Henry's elderly companion wore a troubled look on his gaunt face as he paused to speak to her, "The drive was too much for Mr. Collins," he said. "He had a mild attack on the way home."

Victoria was alarmed. "Have you told Mrs. Stoddard?" He nodded.

"Yes."

"Are you having a doctor?"

Benjamin sighed. "No. He won't hear of it. And he seems somewhat better now. So I don't think we should upset him further by insisting on having a doctor call. I doubt if he could do much and I feel certain the crisis has passed."

"If you are certain," she said dubiously.

"Reasonably certain, judging by past experience with his illness," Benjamin said. "The main thing now is that he have rest and quiet for a few days."

"That should be easy enough."

"I hope so," Benjamin said. "But then, it is not like when we are at home."

And this was confirmed when Roger arrived home later in the afternoon. He at once summoned Elizabeth and Victoria to join Rupert Harvey and himself for cocktails, and after explaining Harvey's peculiar gifts, suggested that they take him up to the hidden room.

"We can't go barging in there today, Roger," Elizabeth said firmly. "Henry is not well and I'm sure it would upset him."

"Rubbish!" Roger said over his martini. "Let him go to some other room of the apartment while we're up there."

"That isn't as simple as you make it sound," his sister said. And with a smile for their guest, who was standing before the fireplace under the painting of the grim Jeremiah Collins, she said, "The old man is resting in that room and he is not well enough to be moved or disturbed for a few days."

Roger took half his martini at a gulp and said, "That means you'll have to spend a while with us, Harvey, if you intend on seeing the room."

Rupert Harvey didn't look upset at the suggestion. "I think that can be arranged," he said. "I have no other pressing business."

"Good!" Roger said.

Elizabeth turned to Harvey with an apologetic air. "I'm not sure the hidden room is all that interesting. In fact, I doubt if you'll consider it worth the wait to see. But perhaps you'll enjoy all the house. It is very old and has many a strange story attached to it."

Harvey smiled. "All these old Maine houses do." He turned to Roger again. "It would interest me to have you repeat what you told me about Henry Collins and that room, if you don't mind."

Roger said, "I don't mind." He sounded hugely pleased to hear the request. At the same time he turned to Elizabeth, who was standing with Victoria. "I suppose you don't approve?" he challenged her.

She told him quietly, "I dislike gossip, whether it has to do with today or yesterday. And what you have to tell Mr. Harvey can be little more than that."

"I don't agree," Roger said, his lip curling in a sneer as he filled his glass again. "I am dealing in facts."

Victoria knew that he would go into the matter, since Elizabeth was asking him not to. The perverse streak in Roger's character would guarantee his crossing her in this. She could only hope that she might hear in Roger's tale some clue to her identity. She was now more surely convinced than ever that she was in some way related to Henry Collins. So she waited with interest to hear what Roger had to say.

Roger said, "I remember the older members of the family discussing Henry first. They spoke in hushed voices as they might of the dead. Of course this was after the tragedy. After he'd had that room from the Ritz Hampton Hotel brought here and carefully reconstructed at Collins House."

"I see," Rupert Harvey said, his face attentive.

"I mentioned Winifred Ray when we talked about this before," Roger said.

Harvey nodded. "The Ziegfield beauty."

"Right," Roger agreed. "Fifty years ago she was the most beautiful of the lot. And she had a remarkably alert mind. She wanted to get ahead in the theater and star in a show of her own. When she and Henry met it was love at first sight for them both. He was a wealthy young man about town with financial interests in various theaters and she was a darling of the rich stage door Johnnies. To all appearances theirs was an ideal romance. No one guessed it would end in tragedy."

Elizabeth interposed with a rueful smile, "I'm sure all this is boring Mr. Harvey."

"Not at all," Harvey said. "I'm enjoying hearing the facts once more."

Roger looked pleased with himself. "But no matter how much my uncle and this stage beauty loved each other, they couldn't hope to marry—for the very good reason that Uncle Henry was already married and had an infant son."

"But he wasn't in love with his wife," Harvey suggested.

Elizabeth interrupted again saying, "Roger is giving you quite the wrong impression, Mr. Harvey. Our uncle did care for his wife and under ordinary conditions would never have looked at another woman. But there were special circumstances. His wife was an invalid. Almost from the day of their wedding she was ill with tuberculosis. And it was a killer in those days."

Roger said, "Exactly. It was one of the great plagues of that period. Henry's wife spent years in the hospital. And he knew early in the game there was no hope for her recovery. Alone and unhappy, he was open to the love offered him by Winifred Ray."

Victoria found herself asking, "What about his child?"

Roger did not seem to find the question odd. He twisted his empty martini glass in his fingers as he replied, "His wife's sister raised the boy. And perhaps that explains why in later years he and the young man were never close. To make things worse, this son married someone Henry did not approve of and he turned his back on him.

Not too many years ago the son died from the same consumption that had killed his mother. Not much is known about what happened to his wife. The old man stubbornly refused to contact her and eventually the family lost track of her."

Victoria heard all this with rising excitement. Roger couldn't dream that this could be terribly important to her. Once again she had hopes that the secret of her parentage might rest with the unhappy old Henry Collins. Had he found out that his daughter-in-law had a child, a daughter? And she was that daughter? It could explain his keen interest in her and the gift of the emeralds.

Rupert Harvey's hollow voice interrupted her thoughts as he told Roger, "It seems to me you're getting ahead of your story. What about Winifred Ray?"

Roger said, "The romance between her and Henry was kept hushed, known only to their intimates. Henry was living in a suite at the Ritz Hampton with Benjamin to look after him. It was there, in the room he later brought to this house, that he and Winifred Ray held their secret trysts. There is no question he was deeply in love with her and planned to marry her when he could."

"But his wife lived on," Elizabeth added, her expression sad.

"Yes," Roger agreed. "Her health ebbing, she still survived, a prisoner in her hospital bed. Months dragged into hopeless years and Henry could still not publicly declare his love for the beautiful showgirl."

Harvey asked, "How did she accept the situation?"

Roger helped himself to another martini. "In the beginning she didn't mind too much. She loved Uncle Henry, and she dreamed of his furthering her career. As the romance turned into a long affair she became restless. But they did not break up. And then the tragic climax came on Halloween night, 1916."

Elizabeth nodded. "I've always thought about it whenever Halloween comes around."

"According to the story," Roger said, after sipping his drink, "Winifred was on her way to a gala masked ball at the Madison Square Roof. Dressed in the costume of a gypsy, she stopped by Henry's suite for a visit. She wanted to let him see her colorful outfit and it was also a kind of reunion for them. She had been away from New York for several months. She stayed with him until she was late for the party and then she left." He paused dramatically. "He never saw her alive again."

Rupert Harvey's face was glowing with interest. "And yet no one really knows what took place on that cold autumn night a half-century ago," he said. "But surely the goblins and evil spirits must have been out in full force. Because, as I recall your story, Winifred vanished as if she had never been on earth."

Roger sipped his drink. "The story goes that Benjamin saw her down the back stairs of the hotel. She always came and left that same way since Henry insisted they avoid any possibility of scandal. He put her in a hansom cab and instructed the driver to take her to the Madison Square Roof."

Harvey suggested, "Couldn't the cab be traced?"

"They tried that," Roger said, "only to find out the cab was involved in a collision with a trolley later that same night and the driver killed."

There was a moment of silence in the big living room. Then with a note of awe in her voice, Victoria said, "So the trail ended with her getting into that cab." As she spoke she could picture the dark street with the horse-drawn cab waiting at the murky side entrance of the hotel, Benjamin coming down with the girl in her colorful gypsy costume and assisting her into the cab's shadowed interior, then giving instructions to the driver seated at the rear. She could see Benjamin stepping back on the sidewalk as the driver flicked his whip and uttered a command to the horse and drove off into the dark October night. Perhaps Winifred Ray had glanced out the window as she left and perhaps not. She might have arrived at her destination, only to fall into evil hands there, or she might have signaled the hackman through the small window at the rear of the cab and given him instructions to take her somewhere else. She could even have come to grief at his hands.

"No one saw her arrive at the Madison Square Roof and she did not return to her apartment that night," Roger said. "The following day she was reported missing and her disappearance became a front page sensation."

"And of course poor Uncle Henry was dragged into it," Elizabeth said.

"Had to be," Roger snapped. "The newspaper people soon dug up information about their long affair and her visit to him at the Ritz Hampton before leaving to attend the costume ball."

Victoria asked, "Did his wife find out about it?"

"As it turned out, she didn't," Roger said. "Her illness had reached the point where she was barely aware of what was going on around her. And within a month of Winifred Ray's disappearance she was dead."

Rupert Harvey laughed harshly. "An ironic twist."

"The newspapers didn't miss that angle," Roger assured him. "They gave poor old Henry a pretty bad time of it. Benjamin acted as his protector and it was then he became the recluse he still remains today."

"But they did find out what became of the missing actress?" Harvey said.

Roger nodded. "Weeks went by. All kinds of wild reports circulated in the press. One paper stated flatly she had been seen in London. Another asserted that she had gone to California to try a movie career. Of course they were both wrong."

"And meanwhile Henry kept to his hotel room," Elizabeth said.

Roger smirked. "Something like you, darling." Going on with the account, he told Harvey, "He blamed himself for Winifred's death. The experience left him a broken man."

Harvey said, "At least he had Benjamin and his son."

"He showed little interest in the boy then or afterward," Roger said. "But he did depend on Benjamin. The family feel Benjamin prevented Henry from taking his own life. The weeks dragged miserably and then on December nineteenth, less than a week before Christmas, the search came to an end. Winifred's body was found in a vacant lot not too far from the hotel. She had been strangled; the motive apparently had been theft. Henry had been lavish with gifts of jewelry to both his wife and the murdered girl. When Winifred's body was discovered it had been stripped of the jewels she'd been wearing on that Halloween night."

"And the police never came up with a definite theory?" Harvey asked.

"The discovery of the body started another round of sensational stories," Roger said. "The most accepted theory was that the cabman was the killer. He had a reputation for wildness and was drunk when he had the fatal accident with the trolley. His death left the case more or less up in the air."

"But surely there were other suspects?" the psychometrist said.

"Many of the papers printed stories hinting that Benjamin might have killed her," Roger said. "They even cast a shadow on Uncle Henry as a possible murderer. But they were ignored as pure sensationalism. Within a few months there were new murders to make headlines and the case of Winifred Ray was forgotten." Roger drained his glass.

"Forgotten by everyone except Uncle Henry," Elizabeth said quietly.

Roger put down his empty glass. "He would never forget. That night was to haunt him all his life. And later when he left the hotel to move into the East Side apartment where he still makes his home he kept the suite at the Ritz Hampton rented in his name. Each month the hotel received its check until they closed. And it was then he bought the room from the wrecking company razing the famous old place and had it rebuilt here."

The account had been a revelation for Victoria. Now she was trying to arrange it all, to see how she fit into the picture. And she could not resist believing that she might be the granddaughter of

Henry Collins, and that he knew it. Now that she knew some of the background she meant to question him as soon as he was well enough. She was hopeful that he might at last reveal the truth to her.

Elizabeth interrupted her thoughts by saying to them all, "Well, it's time for dinner. That is, if you feel like eating after hearing such a gruesome story."

Rupert Harvey came over from his stand beneath Jeremiah Collins' portrait. "I can assure you I'm hungry, dear lady," he said in his sepulchral voice. "And the story your brother told us just now is not by any means as gruesome as many I have heard in the course of my career."

Elizabeth gave a tiny shudder. "Gracious! I can't think of your profession as being a pleasant one, Mr. Harvey."

The deep-set eyes were solemn. "I can be helpful, Mrs. Stoddard," he said. "I feel that in my humble way I have done a great deal of good."

"That must be gratifying," Elizabeth said nervously.

"I have often been able to locate and tell about missing persons," he went on in his hollow voice.

Victoria saw the alarmed expression on Elizabeth's face and remembering the older woman's husband had been among the missing for close to twenty years, she felt that Roger had deliberately put the psychometrist up to saying these things. Desperately she broke in with, "Haven't you ever been accused of being a charlatan, Mr. Harvey? I'm certain many people in your field are just that."

The tall man turned on her angrily. "I use my talents at a professional level. I have nothing in common with the kind of people you're thinking of."

Victoria was at once all mock contrition. "I'm quite sure of that. It just struck me that this must make your work more difficult." She was pleased to note that Elizabeth had recovered her poise and the unpleasant moment had been glossed over.

Elizabeth offered her a wan smile. "You and Mr. Harvey can discuss his work later. Just now I insist we all go to the dining room."

Dinner was not an easy meal. Rupert Harvey had lapsed into a sullen humor and Roger did little to lift him out of it. The burden of the conversation fell on Elizabeth and Victoria and they did their best to cope with it. But Roger was a long way from sober and devoted any remarks he made to sarcastic references to the dark family history.

Leering at his guest, he said drunkenly, "The truth is we all suffer from the curse of the Collins family. Began way back when this place was built and old Jeremiah's wife threw herself over the cliffs. She was the first to go that way! But there were others!"

Harvey frowned. "From the point where the bench is, of course."

Roger was startled. "How did you know?"

"I strolled up that way when I first arrived," the psychometrist said. "I think I told Miss Winters at the time that I could feel the tragedy surrounding the spot."

All eyes at the table were focussed on Victoria and she felt uncomfortable as she said, "Yes. You did mention it."

"You will recall," Harvey said evenly, his piercing eyes fixed on her as if to emphasize his unusual powers, "that I first became aware of tragedy there when I touched my fingers to the bench. I received distinct vibrations that told me the whole story."

"Remarkable!" Roger said with drunken gravity and then gave his attention to his heaping plate.

After dinner Victoria managed to slip away from them. She left Elizabeth and Rupert Harvey talking together, Roger having retreated to his study, and made her way up to the second floor. She went down the corridor to the apartment where Henry Collins was staying and rapped gently on the closed door. After a long moment she heard footsteps on the other side of it and Benjamin opened the door a fraction and peered out.

"Yes, Miss Winters?" he said patiently.

"How is Mr. Collins?"

"Not too well. But he has managed to get to sleep at last. I'm hoping he'll be improved in the morning."

She nodded anxiously. "I hope so, too," she said. "Otherwise you probably should call in a doctor."

"I'll certainly run no risks," the old man assured her.

"I'm sorry to have bothered you," she said.

Benjamin seemed more friendly than he had previously. "You mustn't think of it as a bother," he told her in an earnest voice. "I know how much you think of Mr. Henry."

"I do like him," she admitted.

"He can be a very generous man," Benjamin said. And once again she had the conviction that he knew about the gift of emeralds she'd received from the old man.

"I'll come by in the morning," she said.

"One other thing," Benjamin said. "I'm going up to the roof shortly. I think it will be an excellent night to study the heavens. Why don't you join me later? I'm sure you'd find it fascinating. About ten would be a very good time."

She smiled wanly. "Thank you, Benjamin. I suddenly feel very tired, but if I should be awake at that time I'll surely join you."

"I don't think you'd regret it," the old man said, plainly gratified, and then he closed the door.

She was truly sleepy. But it turned out that sleep did not come as easily as she had thought. The excitement of the day, along with the account of Winifred Ray's murder and the tragedy associated with the crimson and white room on the second floor, had kept her thoughts in a turmoil.

She pictured the fragile old Henry Collins asleep in the bed in that haunted room. And now she began to wonder if she had indeed seen the ghost of the long dead Winifred Ray. Surely she had seen something. But she was still skeptical about apparitions and unwilling to believe her visitor had been from the other side. More likely she had been the victim of someone interested in stealing the emeralds Henry Collins had given her.

Realizing it would be impossible to sleep until she was completely exhausted, she left her room a few minutes before ten and started along the darkened corridor of the third floor level to the door and stairs leading to the captain's walk and the rooftop. She had only gone a short distance when she heard a step in the shadows behind her. And almost at the same moment a hand clutched her arm.

She let out a small cry of terror and wheeled around. In the murky light she saw the tall Rupert Harvey. There was a smile on his gaunt face, a mocking smile.

He said, "So once again I've startled you!"

Sharply she said, "Let my arm go!" And she shook it free of him.

Unperturbed, he remarked, "You'll forgive me for the presumption. I merely wanted to touch you and get your vibrations. I can tell you are very upset."

"Thanks!" she said. "I don't need your fortune-telling!"

He remained calm and collected. "It is somewhat more than that, even if you don't care to admit it," he said. "I know more than you guess."

She stared at him angrily. "What are you doing up here anyway?"

"I assure you I have Mrs. Stoddard's permission," he told her. "She told me I could roam about the house freely."

"I'd say she was making a mistake!" Victoria told him angrily and stalked off in the darkness. She heard his soft mocking chuckle as she went on her way.

She was still upset when she reached the cool silence of the rooftop; she was certain Rupert Harvey meant to give her more trouble.

Benjamin was peering through a giant telescope mounted on a sturdy tripod. He turned to greet her, saying, "Wonderful night for the stars, miss. They're out in all their splendor." He looked radiantly happy as he turned his gaunt old face up to the show of stellar beauty. Victoria at once felt better. "You do enjoy this, don't you?"

"Indeed I do," he said. "And you must take a look through the glass yourself. If you're not interested in the heavens you can look at the village. You can actually read the neon signs on the main street from here."

She laughed. "Aside from the Blue Whale sign there aren't many!"

"It's a strong telescope," the old man said. "Brings the hedge right up to you." And he paused to point out a spot along the hedge that was getting reflected light from the living room windows. He adjusted the telescope and then swung it to her to look through.

She applied her eye to the telescope and to humor him studied the hedge. It was true the strong magnifying power of the instrument seemed to bring the leaves of the hedge within touching distance. It was remarkable even in the faulty light. She was about to swing the telescope toward the stars when suddenly she was aware of a movement in the shadows behind the hedge. A coldness ran along her spine and she could not move her eye from the glass as slowly a familiar figure took shape by the hedge. And she saw the weird phantom of Winifred Ray for the third time!

# CHAPTER 9

FOR A MOMENT Victoria was hypnotized. When the first shock passed she was able to think clearly enough to want to test Benjamin on what she was seeing. Straightening from the glass, she gave him an urgent glance.

"You take a look," she insisted. "It does bring the hedge amazingly close." She hoped the slight tremor in her voice wasn't too noticeable.

"It's nothing new to me, miss," he said mildly. But he did lean down and apply his eye to the telescope as she'd suggested. After a moment, during which she waited with bated breath, he said, "Light's not good. I've known nights when it was clearer."

"You saw nothing unusual, then?"

He showed surprise. "No, miss. Should I have?"

She managed a forlorn smile. "No. I guess not. I was impressed because it is all new to me."

"Now let me show you some of the stars."

Victoria allowed him to tilt the telescope toward the sky and listened politely as the old man gave her a lecture about the various constellations, pausing now and then to allow her to study the star-studded sky through the glass herself. But for her it was all anticlimactic after the vision of the lurking figure by the hedge. She was desperately anxious to get away from the roof and back to her room. She wanted time to think it all out.

At last Benjamin said, "Well, I think that about covers it. I hope it hasn't been too dull for you, miss."

She shook her head. "I enjoyed it. I'm glad you invited me."

Benjamin assured her it was his pleasure and was careful to see her safely down the stairs and along the dark corridor to the door of her own room. She said goodnight, truly grateful for his company, and then went inside.

As soon as she switched on the light she saw that her room had been ransacked once again. This time the search had been more hasty and the intruder had taken no pains to conceal having been there. Her first suspicions were of Rupert Harvey. She was sure he was more charlatan than anything else and if he had any hint that she'd been given the emeralds he'd be after them.

She groaned as she took in the topsy-turvy state of her normally neat room. Drawers had been hastily opened, gone through, and left half-closed with not all their contents returned. Dresses had been taken from the rack in the closet and left on the floor. The bed covering was rumpled, the pillows in disarray and it was clear someone had made a search above and below the mattress.

This time whoever had entered and searched her room had been in a frantic, angry mood. With a feeling of apprehension she wondered if her hiding place for the emeralds had been found, since she was sure it was the emeralds the unknown intruder had been after. Quickly taking a chair, she used it to stand on in the closet. She lifted the loose ceiling board. Then she thrust her hand inside and was reassured as she touched the tin biscuit box.

She drew the tin out and hastily lifted its cover to eye the velvet jewel case inside. Flipping back the lid of the case, she studied the beauty of the valuable emeralds again. As she stared at the four sparkling pieces she couldn't help wondering whether they had once belonged to Henry Collins' wife or to the lovely Winifred, who had met such a tragic fate. She believed they must have been Henry's wife's and he had passed them on to her because she was his granddaughter.

She knew she had nothing concrete to base this belief on, but she continued to cling to it, not only because it explained the old man's actions, but because it promised to make it possible for her to consider marriage one day. Marriage with Ernest, if he asked her. She hoped he would. With this thought she closed the case and then the tin box and restored the treasure to its hiding place. Carefully putting back the ceiling board, she got down from the chair and wearily went about the task of restoring some order to the chaos of her room.

It wasn't until she began to clear the top of her dresser that she came upon the mask. A plain black mask with eyeholes and trailing silk ribbons with which to affix it in place. She had never seen it before and didn't know how it had gotten there. As she stared at it with perplexed eyes she was suddenly aware of a familiar fragrance exuding from it. A faint, rather stale odor of the perfume she had encountered before. The perfume of the hidden room!

Victoria frowned, her mind going back to the story told by Roger earlier. Winifred Ray had been masked and gowned for a costume ball when she had made what was to be her farewell visit to the suite in the Ritz Hampton Hotel on that Halloween fifty years ago! Was this the mask she had worn? And was the faint perfume the same she had used on the night of her murder?

If so, how had the mask come to be here on the dresser? Had it been maliciously put there to frighten her by whoever was after the emeralds? Or had it been brought by phantom hands? She found this hard to believe, as fantastic as the figure she had seen briefly by the hedge through the old man's glass.

Victoria put the mask back on her dresser with feelings of revulsion and fear. It could only mean one thing. Whether living or dead, someone wanted the emeralds and was persecuting her to get them. The one person she could discuss this freely with was Henry Collins. And he was not well enough to talk to her for awhile. Or at least that was what the wily Benjamin pretended. As soon as possible she must see the old man and let him know the danger in which his gift had plunged her.

The following day was warm and sunny. When she came downstairs she learned from Elizabeth that Roger and Rupert Harvey had driven off somewhere together for the day. It had something to do with another house that Harvey wanted to visit.

Elizabeth gave her a questioning look as they stood there in the kitchen. "What do you make of our visitor?" she asked.

Victoria tried hard to be diplomatic. "He is a different sort of person." she said.

"I don't like him," the older woman said bluntly. "He has a sinister air. It could be all part of his pretending. I'm not sure how genuine his claims to psychic powers are." Elizabeth's face clouded. "I think he is probably ninety percent bluff. I can't imagine Roger taking so much interest in anyone of his type who was genuine. I'd say that Rupert Harvey is an opportunist and he's taking advantage of Roger to find out what he can about everyone in the house—with the idea of using it for his own advantage."

Victoria felt in full agreement with what Elizabeth had said. And she remembered how Rupert Harvey had suddenly stressed that he had often located missing persons and Elizabeth's strange reaction to his pointed words. No doubt Roger had provided him with some information regarding Elizabeth's missing husband and he had been prepared to use it against her in some fashion. Perhaps it was part of a scheme to extract money from her in return for his using his talents to find the missing man. Whatever his thought might have been Elizabeth had quickly gained possession of herself and ignored his words. He would not find her easy to deceive.

"I'm inclined to agree," Victoria said. "And I don't think Roger should talk so freely to strangers about his uncle. Surely the old man is entitled to some privacy in his last days."

"Of course you're right," Elizabeth said with a sigh. Her eyes raised toward the ceiling briefly as she considered the fate of the old man resting in that strange room on the second floor. "Whatever happened, it's all past history now. Better unmentioned and forgotten."

"Not if Roger has his way," Victoria said bitterly. "I think he brought this man here to cause trouble."

"It wouldn't be unlike him."

"Last night Harvey was wandering on the third floor. He said you had given him permission to roam around the house. He was quite nasty about it."

Elizabeth registered surprise. "It's the first I've heard of it. He must have misconstrued something I said to get that idea."

"And later when I returned to my room I found that someone had gone through it and messed everything up."

"Do you think it was Rupert Harvey?"

"I don't know. But it certainly could have been."

Elizabeth gave her a penetrating glance. "What could he have been looking for?"

She shrugged. "I don't know." Again she had the impulse to confess everything to the older woman. But remembering how stern Henry Collins had been in his admonition that she shouldn't mention the emeralds until after his death, she remained silent.

"It's not the first time your room has been ransacked. I mean, since the Willards arrived," Elizabeth said. "They are another pair I don't trust."

"I know," she agreed forlornly. And she knew that the Willards could be the culprits, with Benjamin directing their efforts or at least assisting them. She was convinced Benjamin knew about the gift of emeralds and he had invited her to the roof last night and cunningly arranged for her to see the apparition through the telescope. But it was impossible to discuss this properly with Elizabeth without revealing the truth about the gift.

"I'm sorry this has happened," Elizabeth said. "And I'll be glad when we have the house to ourselves again. This summer has seemed endless. It's enough to have to contend with Uncle Henry and his entourage without having that impossible Harvey here! I'm going to speak to Roger about it as soon as they return."

That marked the end of her discussion of the matter with Elizabeth. She went about her morning tasks, intending to go upstairs later and inquire about Henry Collins' condition. But in the meantime the mailman arrived, bringing among other things a letter for her in Ernest's familiar hand. She sat down in the hallway and ripped open the envelope at once, hoping the letter might offer some word about Ernest's anticipated visit in Collinsport.

But she was in for another disappointment. Ernest was not able to get down even for a few days. His schedule had been changed; there would be no intervening time between his tours. His tone of regret was sincere enough and she was certain he felt just as bad about it as she did. He promised that at the end of the year he would take a two week holiday and spend all of it in Collinsport. She studied the hastily-written letter with eyes blurred by tears. The end of the year seemed a long way off at this moment.

She needed Ernest's company and advice. With all the strange turmoil in the old mansion she felt helpless and alone. She had looked forward to this visit of the young violinist she loved. Now he wasn't coming. She couldn't help wondering whether he still cared for her. But a second glance at the letter convinced her that Ernest was also depressed about the way things had worked out.

She heard a footstep and looked up to see Elizabeth standing by her with a sympathetic look on her attractive face. The older woman eyed the letter. "From Ernest?"

"Yes. He's not able to get down here."

"I'm sorry," Elizabeth said sincerely. "He's one person who would be very welcome."

Victoria sighed as she stood up. "There are some letters for you and several for upstairs."

"I'll take them up for you if you like," the older woman said. "I'm going upstairs anyway."

Victoria gave her the letters. "Thanks."

Elizabeth touched her arm. "I know how you feel about Ernest not coming. But he often has little to say about the tour arrangements."

"I realize that," she agreed bleakly.

"Why don't you take a stroll in the sunshine?" Elizabeth suggested. "I'm sure it will make you feel better."

Victoria was by no means convinced that it would, but she did want to get away from the oppressive atmosphere of the old mansion and so she took the advice. Folding the letter carefully, she placed it in the skirt pocket of her light cotton dress and took a leisurely walk in the garden. She had no desire to go near the beach. In her present mood she was certain the ocean's monotonous surge would only deepen her melancholy.

So she found a bench near a bed of rose bushes and sat there with her eyes closed, giving her thoughts free play. Once again she debated the riddle of her identity and felt impatient at not being able to talk with Henry Collins further. Surely the old man would be better after his long rest. And then she heard the crunch of footsteps near her on the gravel walk and opened her eyes to see Benjamin standing by her. The old man presented a strange contrast to the colorful surroundings in his drab gray suit.

He said, "What a beautiful day, Miss Winters."

Victoria nodded. "Yes, isn't it?" She couldn't make up her mind about him. Was he friend or foe? Just now he was the picture of venerable benevolence but she had seen him in other, darker moods.

"I couldn't resist taking a walk."

She said, "Then I assume Mr. Collins is feeling better. That you weren't worried about leaving him alone."

Benjamin looked slightly uneasy. He cleared his throat. "He is a good deal better. I have Molly watching him while I'm out."

Victoria gave him a searching look. "Then he'll surely feel well enough to see me for a little while, later today."

Benjamin Willard frowned slightly. "I suppose so, miss," he agreed with plain reluctance. "Though I wouldn't want you to pay too long a visit. It could set him back."

"I understand," she said, knowing the old man would probably do all he could to keep her from seeing Henry Collins.

Benjamin cleared his throat tactfully. "I see we have another house guest," he said, his eyes meeting hers. "This Mr. Harvey seems a rather odd gentleman. He came into our section of the house last night and was quite insistent on visiting the room in which Mr. Henry was sleeping. I had to be stern in ordering him away."

Victoria smiled. "He's a psychometrist and he's down here on a ghost hunting expedition. I assume the hidden room has a special interest for him."

Benjamin looked grim. "If he disturbs us again I'll feel obliged to complain to Mrs. Stoddard."

"You might find it worthwhile to let him go over the room," she said, offering a stab in the dark to get his reaction. "He is able to infer facts by merely touching objects. Perhaps he could solve some of the unanswered questions concerning the room and Winifred Ray's murder."

The old man looked shocked. "I wouldn't think of taking such liberties without discussing the matter fully with Mr. Collins. And he is in no condition to consider such things." She was certain fear had come into his face. And she recalled that Roger had said the papers had hinted that Benjamin might be the murderer. Certainly he looked guilty now. Was this mild old man a murderer who had gone half a century without paying the penalty for his crime?

There was a moment of tense silence between them. A bee buzzed by them and then settled on one of the rose bushes. Even in the bright sunshine Victoria again felt a hint of the sinister.

She broke the silence by saying, "I think Mr. Collins might be satisfied if he died here in the room that means so much to him. Perhaps that is why he came back here, when he knew he hadn't much time left."

The old man blinked. "It's quite possible. I agree he'd be content to have it that way."

"I heard the whole story from Roger," she said. "Or at least his version of it." She paused. "You must have been the last person associated with Henry Collins to have seen Winifred Ray alive?"

"Why do you say that, miss?" he asked too quickly.

"You escorted her down to the hansom cab."

He nodded. "Yes."

"And she never was seen after she got into it until her remains were found months later in that vacant lot." She was studying the old man's face and it had gone strangely pale.

The old man eyed her warily. "The authorities blamed the cab driver."

"What do you think?"

"I think they were right. He seemed a shady character. I only used his cab because there weren't any others available at the time. I afterwards worried about it."

"Since he was killed later that same evening he couldn't very well deny the charge."

"No!" The reply was offered with brevity that made it clear Benjamin had no wish to pursue the subject.

However, she was determined to query him further. No doubt he had been interrogated by the police many times but that would have been long ago. Now he might be more careless in his answers and she might come upon some clue to Winifred Ray's killer. It was an exciting prospect since she was so greatly concerned with the mystery.

She pressed another question. "I understand she was stripped of her jewelry. I wonder what she was wearing that night? They must have been worth a lot to justify killing her for them. Did you notice when you took her downstairs?"

He was staring off into space and his voice took on a distant quality as if he were actually picturing that long ago night. "Yes, I noticed," he said. "She was wearing a diamond necklace and earrings to match. And Mr. Collins had loaded her fingers with diamonds! His substitute for a wedding ring!" His tone was angry.

"You don't sound as if you approved of the romance?"

"I knew it was bound to end in unhappiness for them both," he said in that same distant tone. "I told Mr. Collins so more than once, but he wouldn't listen. He had become completely enslaved to the girl!"

Victoria studied him perceptively, trying to decide what he must have been like then. Probably as precise in his ways then as he was now, already married and adhering closely to a standard of morality which he felt his master was violating. She could see that he might have disapproved of the wealthy young man whom he served and maybe actually hated the girl who was his mistress. Could such ancient venom serve to throw a new light on the crime?

Very quietly she said, "You didn't like her."

"I knew they were doing wrong."

"Were any of the missing jewels found on the body of the cab driver?"

"No."

"Strange!"

"Not really," he said, glancing at her nervously. "If he took the jewelry, he had probably passed it on to some fence to unload by that time. Or even hidden the stuff away somewhere."

"Or he could have had an accomplice and given them to him. I should think the police would have considered that."

"I don't properly remember, miss," he said, plainly flustered.

She was thinking he might have been the accomplice. He had hated the girl and knew she would be wearing the costly gems. And he had summoned the cab and had it waiting for her. Had he chosen a driver who was in with him on a plot to murder the beauty and steal the jewels?

"The diamonds weren't ever found?" she asked.

"No. The pieces could have been broken up and the stones sold singly. Or they could still be where the driver hid them. He might have been killed before he got them to a fence."

"Assuming the driver was the murderer."

"Who else could it be?" His eyes were fixed intently on her again.

"I can't imagine," she said warily. "At any rate, the tragedy ruined Henry Collins' life."

"He was never a truly happy man," Benjamin said.

"Did you meet his son or his daughter-in-law?"

"Never, miss. They were not close, as you must know."

"So I've heard."

Benjamin changed the subject. "Mr. Collins has taken a great fancy to you, miss." He cleared his throat again. "If you'll excuse me, I should be getting back to him now." He gave a slight bow and turned to walk rapidly away in the direction of Collins House.

She watched him go, still speculating on the answers he had given her. He had been evasive, but she supposed that was natural.

Perhaps the thing that seemed to upset him worst was the presence of Rupert Harvey, the psychometrist, in the house. That suggested several interesting possibilities.

She had a premonition Collins House was about to be the scene of fresh tragedy. Something was going on there that she did not fully understand and she felt herself a pawn in the sinister pattern of events. Were the emeralds the prize that threatened her life?

She was on her way back along the gravel road to the house when Henry Collins' black sedan came rapidly into view. She ducked quickly to the grass, remembering her close call of the other day. As the car drew nearer to her there was a squealing of brakes and it came to a noisy halt.

Jack Willard scowled at her through the open window of the car. "You better quit telling tales to my old man."

Victoria was astonished at his nerve and revolted by his coarse, cruel face. She said, "I don't know what you're talking about."

He leaned his perspiration-streaked face closer to her. "You know, all right."

"I complained about your reckless driving and I could do it again, considering the way you came in here just now."

Jack Willard offered her a nasty smile. "I know what's wrong with you, sister!"

"Oh?"

"Sure! You're sore because I wouldn't give you a tumble. So you got back at me by lying to my old man and this Stoddard dame!"

This was too much! Victoria gave an incredulous laugh. "You certainly have a wild imagination!"

He nodded. "You betcha! I can read dames like you. Well, just watch your step, baby. Maybe you're in more trouble than you tried to make for me!"

And with this strange warning he applied his foot to the accelerator and sped off, scattering gravel. She stood on the lawn, slightly dazed, watching the retreating car. Thus far it had been a strangely upsetting day and she was still tormented by the feeling that something else was soon to happen, something unpleasant that she could not prevent. More than ever she wanted to talk with Henry Collins, to find out what he knew about herself. Surely the old man held the secret of her past.

As soon as lunch was over, Victoria hurried upstairs, anxious to see him while he was still feeling better. Benjamin met her at the door of the apartment and did not look too pleased to see her.

"May I go in now?" she asked.

He hesitated. "Please do not stay long." He waved toward the partially opened door to the hidden room. "He's up and dressed but still very weak."

She thanked him and made her way to the door and opened it. Henry Collins was seated at his rolltop desk. Hearing her, he turned with a bewildered look on his lined face. On recognizing her he seemed less upset and quickly closed a square leather box which was on the desk before him and which he had apparently been examining. Rising with some difficulty, he took a step toward her.

"Please come in," he said, "and shut the door after you."

She did so. "I understood you were ill. I hope you're better now."

He leaned on his cane. "I overtaxed myself taking that drive. But I'm much better. I have wanted to talk with you."

"I'm glad," she said, feeling awkward and hardly knowing how to go on with the conversation. Now that she was alone with him she realized how much depended on this moment.

The heavy red drapes at the window had been partly drawn and only a subdued light entered the high-ceilinged old room. There was an ominous, brooding atmosphere about this transplanted place that increased her fears, and suddenly she found herself wondering if anyone really knew the truth about the crimson room and its tragedy. Anyone other than Henry Collins and Benjamin.

He asked, "Have you carefully hidden my gift?"

"Yes."

He quickly raised a hand. "Don't tell me where. And remember you are not to show them to anyone until after my death."

"Someone has been trying to steal them," she said. "My room has been ransacked twice."

"Impossible!" the old man protested. "No one knows you have them."

"I'd like to believe that, but I can't," Victoria said hopelessly. "My room was turned upside down. And last night I found a mask on my dresser. It smelled of perfume—a perfume that filled this room when I came here one afternoon."

A low moan escaped the old man's lips and he wavered as he leaned on his cane. She went forward to take his arm, but he refused help. "I'm all right," he gasped. "Just a passing spell." And he lowered himself into the chair by the desk. Then he eyed her gravely. "What you've told me suggests you were visited by a ghost. Do you understand me?"

"You're thinking of Winifred Ray, I suppose," she said slowly. "And whoever is trying to get the emeralds and frighten me must have the same thing in mind. For I've seen a ghostly form several times lately. I'm sure it's someone deliberately trying to terrify me."

His head trembled in a palsied motion. "But who?"

"I can't hope to know that unless you give me some more help," she said, kneeling by him. "I think you should tell me everything. Why you have been so kind to me and if I'm really your granddaughter."

He stared at her with troubled eyes. "What gave you that idea?"

She wouldn't be put off now. "Many things," she said. "The gift, for one! The way you've talked. Promising to tell me the truth later. There can only be one important truth for me—the truth about who I really am!"

The old man studied her for a long moment of silence. And she was sure she saw sympathy for her in his wan, lined face. At last, he said, "Just now you said a perfumed mask had been left on the dresser in your room. Several times you have seen what might have been the ghost of Winifred Ray. Can you tell me what she looked like?"

She hesitated. "Tall, with a striking figure. But she wore a large hat and veil. I couldn't see her face."

"You couldn't see her face," the old man repeated quietly. And then he turned and opened the leather box which he'd been examining when she'd first entered. From it he removed a gold locket on a chain and opening the locket, passed it to her. "That is a likeness of Winifred," he said.

Tensely she took the locket and studied the lovely painted miniature inside it. She gave a low gasp. For it was her own face she saw!

# CHAPTER 10

**"I** DON'T BELIEVE IT!" Victoria said in an awed whisper.

"Yes, the resemblance is remarkable," the old man agreed.

Victoria stared at the miniature, unable to take her eyes from it. In a very real sense this was a crushing blow. For Victoria now knew that if she was the grandchild of Henry Collins, her grandmother was Winifred. And since Winifred and Henry Collins never married, their child—her mother or father—was an illegitimate one, born out of wedlock. And yet, wasn't it better to know, once and for all, just who she was—even if it meant finding out that her origins were not all she hoped them to be?

Sighing, Victoria went over to Henry Collins and knelt again by his chair. She felt herself unable to speak.

He placed a hand on her shoulder in a gesture which showed he understood just how she felt.

"Please do not ask me anything about Winifred and yourself. It is not possible for me to say any more at this time, and much too painful," Henry said softly.

Victoria looked up at the lines of grief etched into his face. Although she wanted desperately to pursue the subject, she knew that Henry Collins would not and could not at the moment give her the information she craved. Silently, with tears in her eyes, she handed him back the miniature.

He held up his hand. "No. I'd like you to keep that. I have other likenesses of Winifred. I can spare that one." She looked at the gold locket again, then slipped it into her pocket.

"After a brief silence, Victoria asked, "Was she happy that last night she came to this room?"

He looked at her with mild surprise. "Yes, I'd say so. She was very happy when she arrived. Like most theater people she was a creature of moods, either very gay or very sad. That night was one of her good ones."

"Roger spoke of her having been away. That you hadn't seen her in some months. Had she been away on tour?"

Henry Collins was sitting back in his chair, his thin hands clenching its arms and a thoughtful expression on his wan face. "Yes, I think so," he said absently.

She could see that he had slipped back into the past that he was reliving that night again in his mind. Quietly, hoping not to disturb his reverie, she said, "It must have been good to see her after that separation. You must have been surprised."

"I was," he said, his eyes staring back over the span of years. "I hadn't expected her that night. I didn't even know she was back in New York. Benjamin let her in. She came straight across the room and threw her arms around me. She laughed. Her laughter was like the music of sweet bells; it always enchanted me. She was wearing a colorful gypsy costume of red, orange and black with a narrow black mask and a gold-threaded handkerchief knotted about her hair. It suited her; I thought she was more lovely at that moment than ever before."

"And that was the last time you would ever be together."

"The last time."

Victoria hesitated a moment before saying, "And when she left, it was Benjamin who saw her down to a cab."

"Yes."

"Haven't you often wondered?"

The old man roused himself from his reverie and stared at her. "Wondered what?"

"About Benjamin."

"What about him?"

Victoria didn't know how to go on. But she knew she must, having gone this far. The theory that Benjamin might be the murderer was haunting her and now she must tell it to him.

She said, "Benjamin hated Winifred, didn't he?"

Henry Collins' forehead wrinkled. "*Hated* is a strong word. It would be more fair to say he didn't approve of her."

"He considered her a bad influence on you?"

"Perhaps. But he was wrong. I truly loved Winifred and it was only out of consideration for my wife that I let things go on as I did."

"And on that night Winifred left with Benjamin."

"You keep saying that," the old man told her sharply. "What are you trying to suggest?"

"That Benjamin might have murdered her or at the very least have been an accessory to her murder."

Henry's eyes widened and a look of sheer horror shadowed the patrician face. "No," he said in a tone that was near a moan. "No. I can't believe that. You mustn't think such things. Benjamin has been with me too long! All these years! He wouldn't be guilty of such a fiendish crime."

Henry Collins' face turned gray and haggard. He studied her with despair in his eyes. "You are suggesting that the person closest to me for more than half my life killed the woman I loved?"

"I'm saying it is possible. But even if Benjamin were guilty, you wouldn't consider accusing him and going through the ordeal of a trial that would bring the entire scandal to life again, would you?"

Henry shook his head. "No," he whispered. "Whatever happened, he is safe enough now. I'm not thirsty for vengeance any longer. I only wish that she might be returned to me as she was that night."

"I understand," Victoria said gently. "Forgive me for bringing it up. Besides, his conscience would have punished him enough by this time."

"Indeed you are right," Henry Collins said grimly. "If guilty, he has suffered the weight of his crime all these years. I grant you that should be punishment enough."

"I must go," Victoria said. "I have intruded too long."

"You have been most welcome," the old man said sincerely. "And one last word. Even though you do feel Benjamin may be guilty, I will ask you to say nothing. Let it remain our secret."

She understood how the old man felt and she was warmed by his generosity. Guilty or not, there was no point of turning a man close to eighty over to the authorities.

Hesitating, she drew the locket from her pocket. "Are you certain you want me to have this?"

"Quite certain," he said wearily. "You must keep it." And he closed his eyes.

She left him there sitting in the silence of that room of yesterday looking more like a ghost than a living person. She knew that he could not live much longer. And with his death she supposed the hidden room of Collins House would be padlocked forever, left in deathly quiet, a forgotten corner of the great rambling building to collect cobwebs and spiders and dust. Until in the end its fine drapes would rot, the wallpaper peel and strip, the whole parcel of it give way to filth and decay.

And no one would ever know!

No one would have ever learned the strange room's secret. The murder of Winifred Ray would remain as much a mystery as on that cold December day of years past when her body was found out in the cold. It was a gruesome thought to climax a weird series of events.

When she came down to dinner, Roger Collins was standing in the living room with Elizabeth, the usual cocktail glass in hand, but there was no sign of his guest.

He greeted Victoria with a mocking smile, and to his sister he said, "She does look forlorn, doesn't she? It's easy to tell that Ernest had to cancel his plans for a holiday here."

Victoria said, "I didn't realize I was that easy to read."

"You're a cinch for an expert like me," Roger assured her as he took a sip of his martini. "And wait until Rupert Harvey gets back later tonight. He'll offer you a few surprises."

Elizabeth showed interest. "Such as?"

"He has some things in mind. He's a psychometrist, you'll remember."

"He's dreadful," Elizabeth said. "I wish you'd tell him to go."

"Not until he's finished what he came here to do," Roger said smugly. "When he returns tonight he plans to go over Collins House thoroughly."

Victoria arched an eyebrow and nodded toward the glowering portrait of Jeremiah Collins. "Perhaps he'll be able to once and for all settle the argument about whether your ancestor was a slave trader or not by touching the portrait."

Roger crimsoned. "Don't be facetious!" he snapped and drained his glass.

Elizabeth defended her. "I don't think she's being facetious at all," she said. "It sounds like a good idea and I'd like to see the question answered definitely."

"Deliberately or through ignorance, you're missing the whole point," Roger said angrily. "Harvey can only discover these facts through touching an object that has belonged to some person. Or, similarly, a piece of furniture from a room. It has to be a possession of someone, not a painted likeness of them."

"There must have been physical contact between the object and the person," Elizabeth said.

Roger poured himself a second martini. "Exactly."

"It sounds spooky," Elizabeth said. "I can't imagine why you've invited him here. This place is gloomy enough as it is."

Her brother grinned. "That's one of the reasons the house

interests him. I told him about it and he dotes on these haunted mansions."

"Is psychometry his regular profession?" Victoria asked.

Roger shook his head. "No. He's a journalist. But he specializes in writing up strange events, ghostly appearances, haunted gardens. He's traveled all over the world doing that sort of thing. That's why he came to Maine to do a couple of stories." He paused to grin. "When I told him about Uncle Henry's hidden room I couldn't keep him away."

Elizabeth showed dismay. "But he's a dreadful person! And mentioning the room was hardly sensible. How could you bring him here, knowing he was a journalist? All the scandal surrounding the murder will be brought into the open again. It's not fair to Uncle Henry!"

"From my point of view, Uncle Henry isn't fair to us," Roger said in his mocking way. "There's no possibility of preventing Harvey from coming back here. He's driving down tonight after he finishes with his other client."

So the matter seemed settled. After dinner Victoria felt restless and wanted to be away from the house when Rupert Harvey came back. She was filled with an urge to leave the old mansion for a little while. Elizabeth made no protest about her taking the station wagon to the village, so she went upstairs to get her trench coat from her room. It could be cool driving home even though the days were warm. Maine weather was perverse, even during the summer season.

As she reached the landing, she realized there was someone coming up the corridor from the direction of her room. The night light wasn't on yet, and in the shadowed hallway it took her a second to see that it was Jack Willard. She couldn't think of any reason for him to be on the third floor.

He came up to her brazenly. He was wearing tan sport slacks and a blue turtleneck sweater that revealed his paunch in an embarrassing way. With an insolent smile, he said, "Just taking a stroll around the place."

"Oh?" She didn't conceal her coldness.

"You live up on this floor?" His pretended innocence was exaggerated.

"I thought you knew that," she said sharply.

"I keep an eye on you, honey," he said with a wink. "But not that close. I'm on the second floor, first door off the main hall if you ever want me."

"If I do I'll call your wife."

Jack did a comic cringe. "You've got the sting, baby," he said. "Yes, sir. You really got that little old sting." And with that he ambled off downstairs.

Victoria glanced after him, her pretty face showing her disgust.

She was sure he had been snooping again. Could he have found out about the emeralds some way? Benjamin must have discovered Henry Collins no longer had them and suspected the old man had given them to her.

But Henry had insisted that only he and Victoria knew of their existence. That seemed to rule out the possibility. With a sigh she entered her room. It seemed nothing had been touched. Perhaps this time she had arrived at the right moment and if Jack Willard had intended searching her room she had prevented it. She quickly took her trench coat from the closet and hurried downstairs again.

It was nearly dark when she reached Collinsport. She decided to try the hotel first. It was a good hunch; she found Burke Devlin in the lobby. He excused himself from the man with whom he had been chatting and came over to her with a smile.

"I was thinking about you," he said.

"Things are pretty grim. I couldn't stand it out there tonight."

"Glad that desperation drove you in this direction," the handsome Burke said. "Shall we retire to the pandemonium of the Blue Whale?"

Victoria pushed back a stray lock of her long black hair and rolled her eyes. "I don't know whether I'm up to that clamor or not."

"We can always have coffee here," he suggested.

She eyed the cramped quarters of the coffee shop with distaste. Every word they said would be heard by a dozen pair of ears there. She smiled. "Why don't we just drive down to the dock for a talk?"

"Sounds like a sensible suggestion," he said. "We'll take my car. It's a shade more comfortable." His expensive convertible was the envy of the town.

Not until they had stopped at a deserted spot on the long wooden dock did she relax. She gazed at the lights along the coast. "I wonder if those two small lights way down there are from Collins House," she asked. "I think it should be located just about there."

Burke studied the myriad of lights that dotted the shoreline. "Could very well be," he agreed. "You can see the house from here in daylight."

She smiled at the man in the shadowed seat beside her. "The house has an evil spell. You can't escape it. I come here to get away from it and wind up talking about it."

"Any word of Ernest coming for that short holiday?"

"He wrote. He won't be able to get here until the end of the year."

"That will be long enough." Burke paused tactfully. Then he asked, "Have you two made any plans at all? I mean, is there by any chance a wedding in view?"

She shook her head and stared out the side window at the

water. "Not anything in view. The horizon is bleak."

"Why?"

"Don't blame him," she said unhappily. "It's not his fault that I don't want to make any plans for the future."

"Why?"

Victoria turned to him ruefully. "Just keep on using that single word and we're going to have a grand evening of talk."

"Why?"

"If you must know I'm not eager to marry until I learn something more about this gal named Victoria Winters."

"Oh," Burke said lightly. "I could have said why again just as well. Because I think you're making a big fuss over nothing. Anyhow, hadn't you about decided you were old Henry's granddaughter?"

"That still is a possibility." She gave a small despairing sigh. "But it seems I am never going to find out definitely."

Burke Devlin shifted in his seat as he brought out a package of cigarettes and proceeded to light one. He took a deep puff on it and exhaled thin spirals of smoke. "Be patient. It will work out."

"You can afford to be optimistic!"

"Really?"

"It's easy for you to take a bright view of everything!"

"Why do you speak in that tone?" he wanted to know. "You make it sound as if I'm a man who has everything."

"Well, aren't you?"

"Not quite," he said in a grim tone. "I may be riding high in Collinsport these days, but there was a time when things were different. And not so long ago!"

"I'm sorry," she said, contrite. "I didn't intend to sound envious. You deserve everything you have."

"I won't go into that," he said. "But these last few years have brought a good many changes for me."

"Roger is still terribly jealous of you."

"Really?"

"He's made plenty of remarks about our being friends," she said.

Burke chuckled in the darkness. The end of his cigarette glowed. "Don't let what Roger says bother you."

"I don't," she said wearily. "But everything seems too much right now. I wish the summer was over. I'll be glad when David and Carolyn come back. At least they bring a little life to the place. With them away and that strange old Henry and his equally odd servants there, it's terribly depressing. I don't know how much of it I can stand."

"Any talk of Henry leaving?"

"No. I honestly think he's come back here to die. He looks dreadful. And now Roger has a hateful person as a guest."

"Any new face should be an improvement."

"Not this one," she said. "He's some kind of spiritualist and Roger made a big thing the other night of telling us all about the hidden room."

"And the murder of Winifred Ray?"

"Yes," she said in a surprised tone. "You know."

"When I'm interested, I make it my business to find out things," Burke Devlin said easily. "I had one of my agents in New York dig into the history of the Ritz Hampton Hotel. It didn't take long to discover why Henry Collins clings to that room."

"You should see it!" Victoria said with a small shiver. "It's sort of sinister. And a lot of strange things have happened since it was opened."

"Winifred's murder is an unsolved case to this day."

"I think I know who did it," she said. "I mentioned it to Henry Collins when I talked to him this afternoon."

"Was that wise?"

"I had to get it off my mind," she said. "I think Benjamin killed her." And then she went on to explain her reasons. Burke lit another cigarette as he heard her out in silence.

"It almost makes sense," he admitted. "But if he was guilty, why didn't the police nail him?"

"It was easier to blame the dead cab man. That gave them a closed case."

"Only in a sense."

"At least it took the pressure off them. And just about then America entered the First World War and people were too busy to remember crimes. It all worked out to Benjamin's advantage if he is the guilty one. And maybe that's why he stayed on so long with Henry Collins. To be sure he wasn't ever suspected."

"It's a long shot. But you're placing yourself in danger, making these accusations. If he hears about what you've said, and he is guilty, wouldn't it be logical for him to try and silence you?"

"He knows nothing will be done after all this time."

"You've offered him a written guarantee of that?"

"Of course not."

"Then I doubt that he knows. In fact, on the assumption he is guilty, I can imagine him plotting your murder at about this time."

"You're trying to frighten me!" Victoria said nervously.

Burke Devlin shook his head. "I'm just trying to pound a little sense into you. Stop this loose talk about Benjamin being the killer. In the first place, you're probably wrong and in the second place the story is going to get back to him. You have plenty of problems of your own without taking on Winifred Ray's murder."

"That's what Elizabeth told me," she admitted.

"It was good advice. I'd keep away from Henry Collins and out of his affairs if I were you."

"But you don't understand," she protested. Again she was almost ready to tell him about the gift of emeralds. Instead she said vaguely, "I have reasons for thinking Henry Collins may still be more than just a kind friend. He promised to reveal some secret to me after his death. It could be I'll have to wait until then to find out."

"You don't give up easily, do you?" Devlin said with a sigh.

"Not easily." She laughed. "And now it's time I started back."

The night was dark with the promise of another storm. When Victoria had left the lights of the village behind her, she became very nervous indeed. The narrow road through the woods took on an aspect as menacing as her thoughts. Burke Devlin had given her good advice, she was sure of that. She had made a grave error in allowing Benjamin to think she suspected him of killing Winifred Ray.

And she had made an even worse mistake in openly accusing the old servant to Henry Collins. The old man v/as so feeble and reliant on Benjamin that he might very well confide what she had said to him. And certainly, if Benjamin should be guilty, this would place her in an unenviable position. Old as he was, he might try to kill again.

Worst of all, she was almost a living image of the murdered girl. If Benjamin had hated and murdered Winifred Ray, he must also hate the sight of her since she would undoubtedly remind him of the victim of fifty years ago. She made up her mind to do as Burke Devlin had suggested—have little to do with Henry Collins or his retinue. It was the only wise course. She hoped she wasn't too late in coming around to it.

Thp overhanging branches of the trees closed in on the road ahead. Panic rose up in her. She had never been so frightened of doing this drive alone before. She swung the station wagon around a turn of the narrow, twisting section and suddenly her headlights picked up a heavy log stretched across the full width of the road. She knew she could never get by it; she had just time to brake the car to a halt within a few feet of it. Gasping with fear, she got out of the car, leaving the headlights and the engine on, and made her way to the log. By its size and its position she was forced to the conclusion it had been put there as a roadblock.

But why?

Fog had settled on this section of the road and her answer came as she stood there bewildered in the murky rays of her car's headlights. From a short distance down the road she saw a hazy figure moving toward her.

"Victoria!" Her name was called in that same eerie fashion as in the cellar. "Victoria!" And now as she stared with terror stark on her pretty face the figure took the shape of the phantom that had stalked her so often before—the ghost of Winifred Ray! The big hat and the veil that concealed a face so much like her own. The long, flowing dress and the narrow waistline. Victoria was so frozen with horror she did not even attempt to race back to the protection of the car. The wraith drew closer.

And then she was seized from behind. Strong hands pressed tight around her throat and she stumbled back, struggling and trying to scream. It seemed no use. The strength of her attacker made her resistance a joke. And now she was struggling for breath, the fingers around her neck cruelly constricting. She attempted a last strangled cry for help before she blacked out.

It was the bright light in her eyes that brought her to. At first she thought it must be her car's headlights. But as full consciousness returned she saw it was a powerful flashlight held close to her face. She lifted herself from the gravel surface of the road and stared up to see who held the flashlight.

A familiar sepulchral voice said, "So you've decided to live!"

"Rupert Harvey!" she exclaimed in a frightened voice.

"A late driver, like yourself. I saw your car stopped and left mine to find out what had happened. I discovered you stretched out here."

His presence helped restore her courage, although she realized he might be in on the plot. She said, "This log was blocking the road. I got out to see about it and someone attacked me. You must have seen them."

The face under the slouched brim of the black hat regarded her grimly. "You're the only one I saw. Stretched out in front of your car. Are you certain you didn't faint?"

"Very certain," she said bitterly.

He slid the beam of the flashlight along the log. "We can't get by that. If we both take an end I think we can shove it aside and drive past."

She nodded. "All right."

He chose the end they would move and did most of the work. They barely managed to get it out of the way. He sighed, "Now we can get on to Collins House." He flashed his light over the surface of the road. "Sure you didn't drop anything?"

"I think not," she said, anxious to be on her way.

"One minute!" His tone was sharp and he bent quickly and brought up a small glittering object. "What about this?"

"It's my locket!" she exclaimed. "I didn't miss it." It was the locket with Winifred Ray's painted miniature that Henry Collins had given her.

Rupert Harvey was staring at her oddly. "How do you happen to be mixed up in a murder?" he asked.

# CHAPTER 11

THERE WAS A MOMENT of silence between them as they stood there in the murky glow of Victoria's headlights. The sound of her car's motor, which was still running, was the only noise in the silence of the night.

"Let's not stay here talking," she said. "They'll surely be anxious about me at the house."

Harvey appeared not to hear this. Instead he stared at her with his rather weird, protruding eyes as he retained the golden locket in his hand. And in an even voice he said, "You still haven't answered my question. How are you involved in a murder?"

"I don't follow you!" she protested.

"The locket tells me about it," he said. "You're familiar with my powers in this regard. I've spent enough time explaining to you."

"I'm aware you are some kind of psychometrist."

"That is correct. And I know from handling this locket that there is violent death associated with it." His tone was grave.

Victoria realized she was trembling slightly. "This is not the time and place to discuss the matter. The locket was given to me by someone. And it is true that its original owner was murdered. But not while she was wearing it."

"I disagree," Rupert Harvey said. "Otherwise I would not get vibrations that speak of violence."

"Please let us be on our way," she said. "Whoever attacked me may come back again."

The man in the black hat and coat gave her a doubting glance, but reluctantly he passed the locket over to her. "Very well," he said. "We can discuss this later."

Victoria slipped the locket in her coat pocket and got back behind the wheel of the station wagon. She eased the car around the log and then drove on up the hill at normal speed. The other car followed her. She was still confused and shaken. The roadblock had been deliberately put there by someone who knew she was in the village. She hadn't been able to see her attacker, but her throat still ached from the strength of the massive hands that had savagely attempted to strangle her. And the appearance of Winifred's ghost again had terrified her so much that she had been an easy target for attack.

Had she really seen the wraith-like figure, or was it another case of her taut nerves translating wisps of fog into the outline of the long-ago murder victim? The vision had seemed real enough, but considering all the circumstances she couldn't be sure. It was fortunate that Rupert Harvey had arrived in time to frighten off her attacker and save her life. He was a very strange person and his comments about the locket given her by Henry Collins were causing her new confusion. According to Harvey, Winifred Ray must have been wearing the locket at the time of her murder for him to get the vibrations from it that warned him of violence. But this couldn't be! The murdered girl's jewelry had been removed from her body before she was left in the vacant lot. She remembered Roger telling her this and Henry Collins had agreed with the account. Yet Harvey had correctly identified the locket as being associated with a murder.

Roger Collins opened the front door of the mansion to them. He showed some surprise at their being together and greeted Harvey warmly. "My sister has gone to bed," he explained. "We decided you must have changed your plans and were coming in the morning."

Rupert Harvey removed his hat and coat and gave them to Roger. It seemed to her that the two exchanged glances and she again wondered if all that had taken place on the road was not part of some conspiracy between them. Rupert smiled at her coldly. "My other client kept me later than I expected. It was lucky for this young woman that he did."

Roger's face showed interest. "Oh?"

Victoria quickly gave him an account of what had happened, being careful to omit any mention of the ghostly figure. She ended with, "Thanks to Mr. Harvey, my attacker ran off and left me still alive."

Roger turned to the newcomer. "What do you make of it?"

Harvey shrugged. "I saw no one but Miss Winters. She was on the road in an apparent faint."

Roger Collins went across to the sideboard to prepare drinks. He glanced at Victoria with a frown. "I've told Elizabeth repeatedly she's been wrong in allowing you to take the station wagon into the village by yourself."

"I don't see what that has to do with it," she said.

"It has everything to do with it," Roger snapped. "There are always a lot of youngsters hanging around the Main Street. They're bound to notice you've come in alone. It's an invitation to trouble."

"I've had none before."

"Mere good luck," he told her. "I'd say someone played a practical joke on you—likely some young thugs from Collinsport."

"A practical joke?" she questioned. "My throat will show bruises for days."

"All right," Roger said facing her. "Let's look at it from another angle. These boys know you're driving back alone. So they put a roadblock out and when you leave the car they attack you. We've had cases like that before. And you know it!"

Victoria knew she had gone pale. She felt ill and disgusted. What Roger had said was only too true. There was a certain provocation to the young thugs of Collinsport in her driving to the village alone. They knew she would have to make the journey back along the deserted road. How easy for them to park in the bushes, put out the roadblock and then wait for her in the shelter of darkness.

Rupert Harvey gave her a mocking scrutiny. "I think Roger has come up with the answer," he said. "You've been exciting the town's young hot-bloods!"

"I wish the explanation was that simple," she said.

Roger's eyes met hers. "Then what is your answer?"

She knew it would be useless to try to explain her confused feelings to him and this stranger. Somewhat flustered, she said, "I have none."

His reaction was a cynical smile. He said, "Will you join us in a drink before you go upstairs?"

"Thank you, no," she said, starting for the doorway.

As she passed Rupert Harvey he bowed his goodnight to her and in a low tone said, "We can discuss that other matter tomorrow."

Victoria made no comment but went straight on out and up the stairs. In her own room she examined her throat in the dresser mirror and the heavy red welts she saw on it made her start to tremble all over again.

Of course Roger had lost no time in passing the news on to Elizabeth and when she went down to the kitchen the following morning Victoria found her in a troubled state. Elizabeth left the stove to make a close examination of Victoria's bruised throat.

"This is really too much!" she exclaimed. "I've already phoned the village headquarters of the state police. They've promised to look into the matter, though past experience has taught me we shouldn't take that too seriously."

Victoria said, "It's too bad you did. I don't think raising a fuss will help at all. For one thing. I'm not sure who was to blame."

"I'm sure Roger is right. We have too many young hoodlums in Collinsport. I worry about Carolyn working away from home. It's only that she lives with Mrs. Reid that I allow it."

"Still, Roger could be mistaken," she said.

Elizabeth frowned. "What do you mean?"

Victoria floundered for the right reply. "I mean it could have been anyone."

The older woman said, "That's hardly an improvement on Roger's theory. I'm inclined to believe him for once. It's strictly a case of a lone girl in a car being made the victim of young toughs. You are lucky Mr. Harvey came along when he did."

"I realize that."

Elizabeth sighed and started back to the stove. "Of course, you realize what this means. I simply can't allow you to take the station wagon into town alone anymore in the evenings."

Victoria was really upset by this. "I'm sure it's not that serious. They wouldn't try the same trick twice."

"I'm sorry. I'd worry if I let you go in another night alone. Unless the police discover who is responsible, I'll have to make this a rule." Elizabeth appeared adamant in her decision.

Victoria left the kitchen with a feeling of despair. This was almost the last straw. With Ernest away again she depended on her few visits to the village to keep her in a reasonable state of mind. Burke Devlin had been a tower of strength and had always been ready to talk to her and offer good advice whenever she went in to Collinsport. Elizabeth's new edict would mean she'd be cut off from seeing him in the future—unless he chose to come out to Collins House and visit her. And she doubted very much if that would happen. For one thing, he was very busy and for another, he usually avoided places where he would encounter Roger. It was awkward!

Her work inside done, she went out to the garden. Matt Morgan was sullenly transplanting some roses from one bed to another. She knew that he did gardening only when Elizabeth forced him to, since he regarded himself as the chauffeur and responsible only for the maintenance of the cars. This was ridiculous; it would mean he would be idle seventy-five percent of his time. She avoided the ugly, big man by taking the gravel walk leading to the cliffs.

She had just reached the cliff path when she saw Rupert Harvey coming toward her. He had apparently been up to the point where the bench was and now was headed back to Collins House. He was hatless, but his somber dark suit seemed quite out of keeping with his surroundings on this pleasant summer morning.

As he came close to her he bowed. "How are you feeling, Miss Winters? You had a most unpleasant experience last night."

"My throat is still a little sore," she said.

The piercing eyes fixed keenly on her. "I understand Mrs. Stoddard has informed the police."

"Yes."

"The proper thing to do," he said without much conviction. "I now hope to settle down to making a complete investigation of the psychic phenomena here."

Victoria found herself uneasy in his presence but didn't want to appear rude. "I hope you are successful."

"I will be," he assured her. "I can see that you do not believe in parapsychology. You do not admit to another and more mysterious realm. This place has known much violence and tragedy. I believe the land on which we stand was named Widow's Hill. I intend to convince even such skeptics as you that I can tune in with the spectral world."

"Collins House has always had the reputation of being haunted."

"It is evident to me," he assured her.

She still found it hard to think of him as anything else but a charlatan. Staring at him, she asked, "Are you always able to feel clearly about objects? Tell their history?"

He shrugged. "Sometimes I'm confused. But always there is an explanation." The weird eyes met hers. "About your locket last night. There could be no mistake. The vibrations were too strong. It has been at the scene of a murder."

"Not that I know."

"Then you have not been told the truth," Rupert Harvey said. "I would like to see it again if I may."

"It is in my room at the moment," she said. The truth was, she had no desire to keep the locket with her since he'd linked it with the murder.

"Later, then."

"If you like." There was no enthusiasm in her reply. On an impulse she asked, "Are you able to tell about people?"

His eyebrows raised slightly. "People? In what way?"

"Can you tell about their past?"

Rupert Harvey seemed wary. "If you would care to go into a little more detail?"

Feeling she had nothing to lose by being completely frank, she told him about herself and how she had come to be at Collins House. He listened with interest to her account of being raised in an orphanage and how she now had hoped she might be related in some way to Henry Collins.

When she finished, he said, "Your case history is a striking one. I would like to be able to help you. Do you have by any chance some item that was found with you when you were left at the orphanage?"

She shook her head. "I'm afraid not."

"That presents a problem," Harvey said earnestly. "If there was only a pin, even an old toy, anything that had been left with you, it might serve as a starting point for me now."

"I wish there was something," she said. "I can't think of anything at the moment."

"Perhaps you may have an idea later," he said. "I will always be happy to do what I can. I can understand your frustration in knowing so little about yourself. The unknown always trouble us."

Victoria couldn't make up her mind about the smooth spoken man. He was either miraculously gifted or a clever phony. In either case, he was both intelligent and extremely cautious. She murmured, "Thank you."

Now he was glancing toward Collins House. "Isn't that someone on the doorstep waving to us?"

She turned and saw that it was Benjamin waving in their direction in a clear effort to gain their attention. She also saw there was a state trooper standing beside him on the steps and a police car in the driveway. With a sigh, she said, "I expect it's about last night. The state trooper probably wants to question us."

Rupert Harvey didn't seem dismayed by the prospect. "Of course," he said. "I had forgotten."

They quickly returned to Collins House where the very young state trooper solemnly interviewed them in the living room. He took down both their stories and asked a good many questions. When he'd finished he closed his black notebook and stood up.

"It may take a few days to get anywhere on this, Miss Winters," he said. "The roads are dry and we haven't been able to find any special tire tracks to help us. There are several young hoods in town who might be behind this, but we'll have to sort of eliminate them one by one until we get to the guilty party."

Elizabeth, who had remained standing by the living room entrance during the interview, told him, "Just so long as you make a good try."

"I can promise you that," the young policeman said as he started to leave.

Victoria saw him out to his car, leaving Elizabeth and Rupert Harvey talking together in the living room. She stood in the gravel of the driveway for a moment as the state trooper drove away.

As she turned to go back into the house she was startled to find a haggard looking Benjamin standing between her and the steps. He had made his appearance so quietly she hadn't heard him. The old man's eyes had a strange glint of fear. He said, "What did the police want?"

"It's about something that happened on the road last night. Someone blocked my way."

Benjamin continued to stare at her in the same odd way. "What did you tell them?"

"I couldn't say much," she admitted.

"Do they suspect anyone?"

"They think it may have been someone from Collinsport." She was puzzled by his nervousness and intense interest in the matter.

He nodded, looking less nervous. "They're probably quite right. Something should be done to teach those young village bullies a lesson." He paused awkwardly. "When he first arrived I became very upset," he said. "I was sure my son had been driving on the highway with liquor in his car again. He had some trouble about being found with an open whiskey flask in his pocket before. This time it could mean a permanent loss of his license as a commercial driver. Naturally I felt very concerned."

Victoria smiled. His problem was understandable now that she knew about it. "You needn't worry."

Benjamin was at once brighter. "Thank you, miss," he said and went on across the grass to the rear of the house—no doubt to find his son in the garage and tell him there was no need to worry.

Watching him go, it occurred to her that this would be an excellent time to speak to Henry Collins about the locket and tell him what Rupert Harvey had said about it. She hurried inside and past the entrance to the living room where Elizabeth and the psychometrist were still talking.

Arriving at the apartment in the rear, she went directly to the hidden room, where she thought Henry Collins was most apt to be. She found him huddled in the wing chair before the tall marble fireplace staring disconsolately at the darkened ashes, the remains of the previous evening's log fire.

Going over to him, she said, "May I speak with you a moment, Mr. Collins?"

He looked up at her and managed a weary smile. "Of course. Sit down, my dear."

She took the chair across from him. "I can only stay a few

minutes."

"What is troubling you?" he asked.

She intended to make no mention of her previous night's experience other than to discuss the locket. Leaning forward in her chair, she said, "Last night a guest of Roger's who is a psychometrist examined the locket you gave me. He insists it was worn by someone who was murdered."

His face became grim. "Well?"

"I know Winifred Ray wasn't wearing that locket at the time of her murder or you wouldn't have had it. The thieves stripped her of all her jewelry."

"That is so," the old man said. "And this fellow claims to be able to sense the locket was linked to her murder?"

"To someone's murder," she said. "He doesn't have any idea who it belonged to. I'm dubious of his supposed powers, but there is something about him that frightens me. Yet he has been proven wrong in this instance at least."

There was a long moment of quiet in the crimson and ivory room. Then Henry Collins shook his head. "No," he said. "He has not been proven wrong."

Incredulity registered on Victoria's pretty face.

"I didn't tell you the truth about the locket. Winifred did have it on the night of her death. At least on her person. She had been wearing it before she put on her diamond necklace and earrings. Then she slipped it in the pocket of her costume. The thieves missed it. When the police found her they discovered the locket and in due time it was returned to me."

She listened with an inexplicable chill. It was uncanny that Rupert Harvey should be right after all. She stared at the old man. "Why didn't you tell me the truth in the first place?"

He looked dreadfully weary. "Because of the locket's sad history I felt you would refuse it. I wanted you to have it."

"I see," she said.

"This Harvey must be an interesting man," Henry Collins said in his dry voice. "I must talk with him before he leaves."

"I'm sure he'll want to meet you and see this room," she suggested as she stood up.

The old man nodded. "Yes. This room. I doubt if he has ever encountered another like it."

Victoria glanced about her at the lush other era surroundings and said, "It's like a bridge to yesterday."

"It is yesterday," Henry Collins said sadly. "And that has been my error. I have clung to it so long there is nothing else for me. No present and no future just the tragedy of yesterday. That is all I have left."

She was touched by his loneliness. "There are many people who depend on you," she said. "Benjamin and his family. And I'm sure Elizabeth would feel bad if anything happened to you."

She hesitated. "And so would I."

For the first time his haggard old face brightened. He managed a fleeting smile for her. "That is kind of you, my dear. You are so very much like her in looks. When I see you I almost feel it is Winifred beside me." He gave a sigh. "What tricks time plays. The troubled laughter of time. If she were alive today she would be in her seventies. An old woman!"

"I'll be back to see you again," she promised.

"You are always welcome," he said, almost at once lapsing back into his reverie and paying no attention to her as she left the room.

She went downstairs in a distressed state of mind. Seeing no one, she made her way along the hall to the study. Elizabeth wasn't there, so she went in and closed the door. Then, assured of temporary privacy, she called Burke Devlin in Collinsport. He happened to be in his room at the hotel so she was connected with him immediately.

"I know what happened last night," was the first thing he told her. "The police are working on it."

"I thought you'd hear," she said. "It means I'll not be able to drive in again at night. If we're ever to meet you'll have to come out here."

"I'm quite willing to do that for the pleasure of your company," the man at the other end of the line said. "I can drive there for you and bring you back to the village whenever you like."

"Thanks," she said. "I don't feel so much like an exile now. I'm phoning because I have a problem."

"Such as?"

"It's about a locket," she said. "I've heard several stories about it. I'm not sure which is correct. According to my information, the locket was found on the body of Winifred Ray when it was found in the vacant lot. I have a feeling I haven't been told the whole truth. I know you've had an agent looking into the records of the case and I'd like you to check and see if there was such a locket and if the police did find it in a pocket of her dress."

"That shouldn't be too hard," Burke Devlin said. "It may take a few days. I'm not sure I should do it for you. I warned you against probing into the Ray murder further."

"This is just for my own information," she insisted.

"I hope you're being truthful," he said, dubiously. "I'm not certain."

"Just find out for me, please!" she urged before she hung up.

Somehow talking with Burke and enlisting his aid in the

matter made her feel better. She knew he would find out all the details, and she was anxious to clear it up to her own satisfaction. With this looked after, she went upstairs to change into a dark blue dress for dinner. She was finishing her hair when the knock came on her door. A soft and hesitant knock.

Going across, she opened it to discover Rupert Harvey standing there. He bowed. "Forgive me. I've been impatient to look at that locket again."

She stood in the doorway, not eager to let him in. "I was on my way down to dinner."

"Fine. We can go down together after I have seen the locket."

There seemed nothing to do but humor him and get it over with. She stood aside and said, "Come in."

He did so, his piercing eyes seeming to take in every detail. "What a friendly old room," he observed and stood waiting for her to get the locket.

She had it in a top drawer of the dresser. And now she brought it out and came over to him with it. He took it with a slight frown and after studying the outside case he snapped it open. For a moment he stared at the miniature. Then he whistled softly and raised his eyes to her.

"I'd almost say this was you."

"It was done years before I was born. It's someone whom I resemble. That's why the locket was given to me."

He nodded without replying and then closed the locket and held it up to his temple. He shut his eyes as if concentrating. She watched his performance with growing uneasiness. At last he opened them and lowering the locket, offered it back to her.

"No doubt of it at all," he said. "Murder! Absolutely!" And as he spoke the keen, protruding eyes scanned the room again to rest on the closet door. They then lifted as if they were focused on the shelf and the hidden spot where she had put the emeralds. He smiled faintly to himself. Then turning to her, he added, "A most fascinating experience. I thank you, Miss Winters. Now may I accompany you down to dinner?"

Roger had had more than his usual quota of martinis before dinner and was in one of his most expansive moods by the time they all sat down. Almost at once he told Rupert Harvey, "You'll be pleased to hear my respected Uncle Henry is feeling a good deal better. I hope tonight to be able to show you his room."

The stern face of the psychometrist lit up. "I've been looking forward to that," he said. He was apparently not going to let on he'd been up there on his own before.

"Well, Henry Collins ought to welcome you," Roger went on drunkenly. "Not that I'm certain he will. He and Elizabeth seem to think this is something to keep from you. I disagree. It's your type of thing, not a replica, but the room in which he met that girl. He had it removed in sections from the Ritz Hampton Hotel before it was torn down and had it brought here. My father gave a portion of the house to him for the project."

Harvey's piercing eyes were bright with expectation. "Of course you must show me the room after dinner."

"I intend to," Roger assured him.

From the head of the table Elizabeth appeared nervous. "I'm not sure that Uncle Henry will welcome visitors," she said.

"It is our house!" Roger retorted as if that settled it.

Elizabeth compromised by summoning Benjamin after dinner and asking if they all might go up and visit the room a little later. Rupert Harvey was plainly excited at the prospect and Victoria found herself wondering how it would all turn out.

A little after eight-thirty Benjamin came down and said the old man would be glad to welcome them to the room before he retired. They followed the elderly man upstairs, with Rupert Harvey making complimentary remarks on the excellence of the venerable mansion to Elizabeth. Victoria trailed in the rear already a little apprehensive.

Darkness had come and the light from the ornate chandelier in the hidden room bathed everything in its soft yellow glow. Henry Collins was seated in the same chair where Victoria had left him and looking extremely weary. He apologized for not rising and complained of not feeling well. Roger introduced him to the psychometrist, who was plainly thrilled by the transplanted room.

"It's incredible," he said. "This room actually has its own mood. Different from all the rest of the house."

Roger was standing before the fireplace with a brandy provided by Benjamin. He said, "I suppose it has the atmosphere of its parent body, the Ritz Hampton."

Rupert Harvey showed a strange awareness. "I sense something here," he announced. "Something peculiar to this room."

Elizabeth was seated in the chair across from the old man. She said, "When Uncle Henry is not here, we always keep this room locked. That is how it has come to be known as the hidden room."

Benjamin stood behind her, his eyes on his master. His lined face showed concern for the old man in the chair. It was almost as if he felt this excitement was too much for him. Victoria, standing near the ailing Henry Collins, was of the same opinion. She thought Roger might have spared his uncle this cruel ordeal.

Rupert Harvey had been standing in the center of the room with his hands pressed over his eyes. Now he lowered them. Appealing to Roger, he suggested, "As part of an experiment, would you kindly have all the lights in the room switched off for a moment?"

Henry Collins reared up a little on the silver-headed cane and frowned at the psychometrist. "Just what have you in mind, sir?"

"This room is remarkable," Harvey said. "It is almost speaking to me. The lights out, please. It will help me catch the vibrations!"

Roger didn't wait for Benjamin to act. With a derisive smile he went over and quickly switched off the chandelier himself. An eerie darkness fell on the room with just a narrow band of moonlight striking Rupert Harvey so they could all see him standing there concentrating. Motionless with his hands pressed to his eyes once more.

Then he began to speak in a high-pitched, nervous manner. "Yes, yes," he said hastily. "Yes, I have it. Great agony! Hatred! Anger! A scream!" His voice had been growing louder and now as if in pain himself he cried out, "I feel murder in this room!"

He had no sooner uttered the words than Victoria heard a soft moan from the old man in the chair beside her. Panic welling up within her, she screamed, "The lights! Quickly! Something's wrong!"

# CHAPTER 12

It seemed an age before Roger flicked the lights on and by that
time old Benjamin had found his way across to his master in the
darkness. He was now kneeling by the stricken Henry Collins who
lay back in the chair, apparently unconscious.

Elizabeth turned to her brother. "Phone the village! Get the
doctor here as soon as you can!"

Before Roger could start for the door Benjamin turned
to them all with a cold look on his gaunt old face. "It will be the
undertaker you should call, not the doctor!"

"No!" Victoria's voice was anguished.

"Yes, miss," Benjamin said quietly, his head bowed. "Mr.
Henry is dead."

Elizabeth touched a hand to her temple and turned away.

Roger stood there looking abashed, while Rupert Harvey
seemed to have regained control of himself and now stood in a
kind of daze staring at the corpse.

"The excitement was too much for him," Victoria said, tears
gathering.

Benjamin did not lift his head. "Yes, miss," he agreed in a
low voice.

There was a long moment of silence. Then Roger said, "Well,
this is a fine thing to have happen here! It's too bad he couldn't

have hung on until he got back to New York! Now we'll have all the fuss and bother of a funeral!"

"Roger!" It was Elizabeth reprimanding her brother sharply. She turned to Benjamin. "Come with me, Benjamin, and we'll start looking after the necessary details."

So began a trying and depressing three day period. Elizabeth quietly took charge and things went smoothly. She informed the old man's New York lawyers and one of the well-groomed members of the firm flew to Collinsport to attend the funeral. For Victoria it was the beginning of a time of ordeal. She was torn between a desire to tell Elizabeth about the emeralds and a feeling that she should wait at least a few days after the funeral.

It was appropriate that it should be dark and rainy the afternoon of the funeral. Dressed suitably in black, Victoria paused on her way downstairs to the final service, which was to be held in the living room, and made her way along the dark corridor to the apartment. She entered the hidden room, especially quiet and gloomy on this rainy afternoon, and stood there amidst the shadows. She could make out the outline of the chair in which he had died. And then her eyes moved to the ancient rolltop desk at which he had been seated the day he'd given her the locket and revealed her likeness to the murdered Winifred.

Now it was all over. Soon this room would be sealed off again and probably forgotten until the entire structure was finally razed by fire or leveled by a contractor's bulldozer. It was as dead now as the old man who lay in his casket downstairs, because no one any longer remembered or cared.

She heard a board creak in the near darkness behind her and turned startled eyes to see Benjamin standing there in sober black. The old servant looked ravaged by grief.

She said, "I came here because this is where I'll always picture him."

Benjamin nodded. "This room meant everything to him, miss."

"His life didn't end the other night. He died when she did all those years ago."

The servant looked at her uncertainly. "Yes, I suppose we could say that."

"It is the truth."

Benjamin said, "You would know. He talked to you more than anyone else in the last weeks. Because you looked like her, he was ready to confide in you."

"Yes," she agreed. "He told me a great deal."

Benjamin frowned. "I expect now the most of it will be better forgotten. You're too young to live in the past as he did, miss."

"I'll try not to," she said with a sigh. "But there are some things that can't be forgotten." She paused. "I suppose we should go down and join the others."

"Yes, miss," he said and stood aside for her to lead the way.

The funeral party was small and strangely assorted. Besides the officiating clergyman and the undertaker and his assistant there were only the members of the family, the lawyer from New York, an unhappy-looking Rupert Harvey and Burke Devlin. After the service Burke paid his respects to Elizabeth, who would not be going to the small village cemetery where Henry was to be hurried. Then he drew Victoria aside.

In a low voice he said, "There seems to be something strange about all this."

"Roger's responsible for the old man's death," she said bitterly. "He brought that weird psychometrist here. The night of Henry's attack he put on a mad kind of performance in the hidden room."

Burke glanced across the room at the tense, hawk-faced Rupert Harvey. He murmured, "Sure is an odd type. I'd keep strictly away from him."

"I intend to."

"I'll drive you to the cemetery in my car," Burke said, taking her arm and leading her out into the rain.

As they followed the funeral cortege Burke said, "I put my man in New York to work on that locket business. I should have word tomorrow. I thought I'd come by here tomorrow night."

"Please do," she said.

"I may be a little late," he went on. "And if business holds me up too long I'll come the next night."

"It won't matter," she said. "Things will be even more deadly dull than ever with the old man gone."

"What about Benjamin and his son and daughter-in-law?"

They were in the wooded section now and she stared out the window at the driving rain. They were passing close to the spot where the roadblock had been and where she was sure she'd last seen the phantom figure of Winifred Ray.

She said, "They'll be staying on here a few days to pack things up and prepare to go back to New York. I imagine they'll clear out the apartment there and then be dismissed by the estate."

"No doubt the old man will at least leave Benjamin well provided for," Burke said as the procession slowed for the hill. "He was very wealthy, wasn't he?"

"I think so," she said. Turning toward him, she asked quietly, "Burke, did you ever see a ghost?"

He stared ahead of him, his eyes on the hard-working windshield wiper, and didn't answer her for a moment. Then he said, "You want an honest answer?"

"I suppose so."

"I'm not sure."

"Neither am I," she said and stared out the window at the rain again.

Burke sighed. "What, may I ask, brought that on?"

"I'll explain it to you tomorrow night," she promised. "It would take too long now. And anyway, it isn't the time." She intended to tell him about the emeralds Henry had given her and the appearances of his lost love's ghost that had followed. But she felt the following night would be soon enough. They drove on to the cemetery in silence.

When they arrived back at Collins House, Roger made a beeline for the sideboard in the living room. "I don't know about the rest of you," he said. "But I need a good stiff drink."

"I'll join you," Rupert Harvey said with a shiver. "I normally avoid all funerals. I'm much too sensitive."

"This one was a lulu," Roger said, pouring himself a stiff one. He glanced at Victoria. "What about you?"

"Sherry, please," she said quietly and sat down. She felt chilled from standing in the rain.

When they all had their drinks Roger took a position in the center of the room and gave Rupert Harvey a jeering smile. "I promised you plenty of spooks if you came to Collins House and I think I've kept my word."

Rupert Harvey took a gulp of his drink. "You have indeed," he said. And the piercing eyes held a troubled glint. "I have the feeling your sister thinks I hastened the old man's death and now resents my remaining here. I'll leave in the morning."

"No need of that," Roger protested.

"I prefer to," the other man said.

"Victoria doesn't blame you for Uncle Henry's death, do you, Victoria?"

She met his glance evenly. "It's past time for politeness. I think Mr. Harvey did upset the old man and brought on his attack."

Roger scowled. "I might have known you'd agree with Elizabeth."

Rupert Harvey came over to her and she was alarmed to see that he was trembling and in a state of rage. He pointed an accusing finger at her, "Let me tell you something. I think Henry

Collins is dead because he was involved in a murder and he knew I had found out."

She stared at him incredulously. "Winifred Ray wasn't murdered in the hotel. Her body was found in a vacant lot."

"I can't help where her body was found," Harvey said angrily. "That room screamed to me of murder! And when I said so the old man had his attack."

"You see," Roger said, "everyone has his own theory. I say, forget it!"

Victoria felt she should defend the dead Henry Collins if only because of his kindness to her. She rose, saying, "I might believe your story, Mr. Harvey, if I hadn't known Mr. Collins and heard him again and again express his deep love for that girl. I know he wasn't involved in her murder." She put down her half-empty glass and left the living room to them.

Before she went to sleep that night she moved the chair to the closet and stood on it to make sure the emeralds were still in their hiding place. She would not have to keep them a secret much longer. Tomorrow night she would tell Burke Devlin about them and give them to him to put in his safe at the hotel. Then she would let Elizabeth and the others know of Henry Collins' generosity.

She felt that whoever had ransacked her room before in search of the emeralds would be likely to come back again. But once they knew Burke had them it should remove her from danger. She thought that Rupert Harvey guessed something about them through his powers. Certainly those piercing eyes had sought out the closet when he'd been in her room and he had stared at almost the exact spot where she had hidden the emeralds.

The psychometrist's attack on Henry Collins had not shaken her faith in the old man. She had told both him and Roger what she felt. She didn't think Henry Collins, the man who might be her very own grandfather, would have ever been capable of murdering anyone. And all the facts indicated that Winifred Ray had been murdered away from the hotel. There was just one thing that troubled her—the locket. Henry Collins had lied to her about it and then changed his story. This had bothered her at the time and it still did. But she hoped Burke Devlin would throw light on this puzzling question when he received his report from New York.

Sleep came with difficulty. And when she did drop off into a fitful slumber it was filled with fantastic nightmares in which Henry Collins and a fanatical Rupert Harvey played leading parts. They were too jumbled for her to have any clear memory of them in the morning. But she knew they had been terrifying.

The weather changed again; it was fair and warm the next day. The only event was the departure of Rupert Harvey. He said good-by to no one, but drove off quietly early in the morning. It was revealing that everyone was relieved. His presence had been like that of a grim vulture in the old mansion.

Benjamin and the others were busy packing and so Victoria had little contact with them. She did have a fairly long chat with Elizabeth when they finished work that afternoon. Seated in the rear sunporch the regally lovely mistress of Collins House got around to the subject of Henry Collins again.

"I do feel some blame in his death," she said. "I should have stopped Roger and his half-mad friend from going ahead with their visit to the room. I'm positive Rupert Harvey's mystic powers are nothing but sheer bluff."

"I wonder," Victoria said. "I'm sure he was right in some things."

"Things which he found out about by carefully listening to our conversation," Elizabeth said angrily. "The rest was a brazen display to work on the superstitions which we all share, whether we care to admit them or not."

"I suppose you are right," she agreed. "In the end he said that your uncle died because he was about to reveal him as a party to a murder."

"Sheer nonsense!" the older woman scoffed. "Uncle Henry was ill when we came to the room, too ill to get out of his chair. He even challenged Harvey before Roger took it on himself to switch off the lights. It was a seizure that killed Uncle Henry and sheer coincidence that it should happen as it did."

"He was very old and ill," Victoria said. "He knew he must die soon. It was mercifully quick."

"I comfort myself with that knowledge," Elizabeth agreed. "I believe the time had come for Uncle Henry." She paused. "I have had an initial look at his will and I found it somewhat surprising."

"I suppose he worried about Benjamin," Victoria said.

"Yes. He was very specific about him. The world had changed a great deal since Benjamin came to work for him. And so had Uncle Henry's fortunes. But that is something we needn't worry about yet."

That ended the discussion and Victoria began to look forward to the evening and the arrival of Burke Devlin. A strange feeling of foreboding had taken hold of her again and she had a conviction that more tragedy was to follow in the old mansion.

Darkness had come and she was standing out in the warm night, hopeful that the headlights of Burke Devlin's car might show any minute. He would have to come soon if he was going to. It was already late enough for Elizabeth to have gone upstairs to bed and Roger was in the study doing some hard drinking.

She needed him. A difficult day had been followed by a more difficult night. And she had not been able to shake off the feeling of depression that had strangely taken possession of her. She was aware of someone on the porch beside her and turned to see old Benjamin.

The old servant said, "I'm taking down my telescope and other equipment tonight. It's a wonderful night for stars. The heavens are filled. I thought you might enjoy a last look at them."

She smiled at him, sensing the loneliness Benjamin must also be feeling for his late master. And as it was no longer likely that Burke would come, she felt she should escort the old man to the captain's walk as a gesture of consideration. She said, "I was expecting Mr. Devlin. I have some things to tell him. But I don't think he's coming tonight. I'd enjoy seeing the stars again."

And she went up the several flights of stairs with him, asking polite questions about his hobby and trying to show an intelligent interest in it. When they did reach the dark roof the stars took on an extra brilliance.

Victoria let the old man adjust the telescope for her and then scanned the sky with it. After a moment she turned to him with a smile. "When I was a child at the orphanage we were convinced that when a person died they became a star. And that somewhere up there were stars watching us and protecting us, who were our parents." She paused, her eyes shining at the memory. "It was a lovely thought and a comforting one. Too bad the harsh realities overtake us so soon and we become grown-ups with no magic left."

He was standing in the shadows so she could not see his face clearly. In a low voice, he said, "Yes, miss."

She glanced toward the stars again. "I'd like to think of them up there, Henry Collins and the girl he loved. Somewhere together. Surely she became a shining lovely star up there just as she was here on earth!"

"No!" It came as a hoarse, strangled outburst from the old man.

She turned to him in surprise and saw hate distorting the gaunt old face. "What is wrong?"

"You need taunt me no longer," he said. "Just seeing her face in yours all these weeks has been torture enough! I know what you planned to tell Burke Devlin tonight. You were going to tell him about the emeralds Mr. Henry gave you!"

She was caught unawares. "He told you he'd given them to me!"

The old man's sarcastic smile was reply enough. "No. But I guessed right away. I've been certain of it ever since that day he sent me from the room. He knew he was going to die soon and his conscience was bothering him. So he gave you the emeralds and told you the truth about his precious Winifred Ray! He murdered her and I helped!"

Victoria gasped and drew back. "He murdered her!"

"I hated her from the beginning and that night I was glad to see it over with."

Horror flooded her face. "You're telling me that he murdered her! In the room that's downstairs now! And that you were also a party to it!"

"I warned him against her. I told him a pretty face often conceals the heart of a witch. But he was beyond listening to any advice. All he could think of was her!"

"He killed her!" she whispered, shrinking back to the railing.

He followed her. "Yes, Henry Collins was a murderer. Locked his two hands around her throat," he said grimly. "She'd been away for months. Pregnant by him, she claimed and she'd gone off to have his child so there would be no scandal. It was planned to have the child taken care of by a country couple until the death of Mr. Henry's wife. The poor dear saint was near her last with TB! And him carrying on with that Jezebel who wasn't worth her little finger! Who had nothing but a pretty face! Your pretty face!"

Victoria was breathing hard. "He said you hated her!"

"I did!" Benjamin said harshly. "They planned to marry as soon as his wife was dead and then Mr. Henry would adopt the child as his own. But that slut had no intention of marrying him. She came to the hotel room that Halloween night to tell him so and taunt him! She was drinking and she blurted out that she'd given the baby away for adoption. It was like spitting in Mr. Henry's face. I had never seen him in such a rage before. I was watching and listening to it all from the other room, waiting to escort her to a cab to be taken to the party. When she told Mr. Henry that, he called her by a name I had never heard him use before and which was proper for her! Then he said it had been his money she'd wanted and she was welcome to it since she'd earned it in the usual way. And he slapped her hard across the face and turned his back on her!"

He paused, his gaunt old face working with rage. "She had never expected it from him. She had thought him a fool but he was a gentleman. She cursed him and then she turned and ran over to the dresser and picked up a paper knife we kept there. I knew it was long and sharp and a weapon to kill with! I saw her go close and lift it to plunge it in his back and then he wheeled around and gripped her by the throat! When he finally let her go she fell at his feet. She wasn't pretty anymore. And she was dead! Mr. Henry wasn't able to think or do anything. So I was the one that had to strip the emeralds off her, find a way to get her out of the hotel and hide her body in a vacant lot."

"But he didn't deliberately murder her!" she said. "He killed her to save his own life. And you only helped get rid of the body."

He nodded. "But from that moment on, the two of us were caught up in a trap of lies and evasions that were to last all our lives. I would never tell. But I knew from the first that he might decide to one day. So I could never leave him. And when he met you and you reminded him so much of her I got the feeling you would be the one. That he'd give you the emeralds and tell you the truth, just as he did!"

"You're wrong!" she protested. "He kept his secret even though he did give me the jewels!"

Benjamin's gaunt old face was unrelenting. "You expect me to believe that? I know what you intend to tell Burke Devlin! That I helped him! And I'm still alive to be turned over to the police! But I won't let you, Miss Winters! Not after all this time!" His words were spoken in a low, hoarse voice as he came close to her.

She knew what he must have in mind. She was going to accidentally fall from the captain's walk. And she had no doubt he was insanely fearful to the point where he'd have no trouble carrying his plan through. She edged away as he drew constantly nearer. And then she eyed the big telescope on its tripod with careful calculation in her frightened eyes. As he made a lunge toward her she grabbed the thin end of the telescope and whirled it up and around so that the heavy end hit him full across the mouth. He staggered back, his hands wildly clawing the air and tumbled over the railing of the captain's walk!

Victoria screamed, her hands pressing to her mouth, her eyes widened with horror, as in a kind of nightmare she watched him roll over the gradually slanted shingles. Then just at the edge of the long drop to the ground, the body of the old servant came to a precarious halt.

She heard footsteps on the stairway, then the door was thrown open and Burke Devlin came out onto the captain's walk. He quickly took in what had happened and lost no time in climbing over the railing.

"I'll get him," he promised. And somehow he did manage to drag the old man back to safety. Benjamin still lived, but he was badly injured.

When Jack appeared on the scene he insisted with drunken indignation that he drive the old man to the hospital at Ellsworth. The doctor in Collinsport was away and it was their best bet. Burke reluctantly agreed and they followed the careening car up the narrow wooded road and to the main highway leading to Ellsworth and the hospital there. It was a drive she'd never forget. Burke, grim-faced at the wheel of his big convertible, had her fill him in on the details as they made the journey.

By some miracle they all arrived at the hospital without an accident. Benjamin, who had not recovered consciousness, was quickly given treatment and installed in a private room. A somewhat sobered Jack Willard and his overwhelmed wife made known their decision to remain at the hospital for a time. When the doctor in charge of the case advised Victoria there would probably be no immediate crisis in the patient's condition she agreed with Burke that she should return to Collins House.

On the drive back, Burke said, "Now that you know the murderer was Henry Collins, what are you going to do?"

She stared at the dim lights of the elaborate dash, perplexity showing on her pretty face. "It's all happened so quickly! And it's so awful I don't know that I've made up my mind yet."

He kept his eyes on the road ahead. Very casually, he said, "You could wait to see if Benjamin lives or not. If he dies your information won't have much importance to anyone."

She nodded slowly. "No. I guess that's what I'll do. I've been thinking. And I'm sure. I have the answer. The child Winifred Ray gave away for adoption must have been my mother or even possibly my father. That explains so many things. My receiving money from down here and their ultimately having me come here. Also my resemblance to Winifred Ray."

He gave her a look of ironic amusement. "You're not fussy about who you pick for a grandmother, are you?"

Victoria shrugged. "I can't help it if she was a horrible person who let Henry Collins down badly. At least she was beautiful. And from everything I've heard there doesn't seem much doubt about the relationship. Henry must have known. Also Benjamin. Even if he should recover enough to talk I doubt that he'd tell me. That old man hates me as much as he hated my grandmother!"

"Your possible grandmother!" he corrected her.

Yet Victoria was stubborn in her certainty her guess was right. She didn't confide her thoughts on the subject to Elizabeth or even mention the emeralds. Before bringing everything into the open she wanted to see how Benjamin would be. He remained unconscious for twenty-four hours and the doctors seemed to agree he had little chance to live.

Then, on the following morning, she received a call from the hospital. It was Jack Willard and he said, "Dad is conscious and he's talked a little. He keeps asking for you. He's still in bad shape but the doctor thinks he might rest better if you came to see him."

"I'll be there as soon as I can," she promised. The drive to Ellsworth had never seemed longer and all the way there she prayed he would still be alive when she reached the hospital. She was certain that at last she would know the truth.

The nurse ushered her into the silent, pale green hospital room. Benjamin looked as if he had already breathed his last. His eyes were closed, the gaunt face a parchment white. The nurse made a sign for her to wait and then went over and in a soft voice told him, "Miss Winters is here."

After a torturing moment his eyelids twitched and opened. The nurse gestured her to approach his bedside. As she did so Benjamin's pale blue eyes turned and focused on her. His lips moved restlessly and he seemed to be whispering. She bent close to him.

In a low whisper, he said, "I was wrong. Wrong to try and steal the emeralds from you." He paused. "Needed money. Jack heavily in debt to gamblers. The emeralds would have solved it all. Jack and his wife helped me. Molly played the ghost! Harvey came to spoil plan!"

She said, "I understand. You needn't explain. One thing I must know. Was Winifred Ray my grandmother? Am I the daughter of the child she had by Henry Collins and which she gave away for adoption?"

The old man closed his eyes again and she had a moment of fear, certain that he must have sunk into unconsciousness once more. But it seemed he was marshalling his small strength, for now he looked up at her and began whispering weakly, "The child died at birth. I found that much out later. She had lied to him, thinking she could use this as a hold over him and get more money if she ever needed it. I decided it was kinder not to ever tell him about it. All he had left then was the dream picture he'd built of her and through the years he clung to it."

Again Benjamin closed his eyes and this time he did not open them. The short effort had exhausted him. The nurse nodded for her to leave. With a sigh, Victoria turned and went out. There was nothing left to stay for. Benjamin had answered her question. She was not even an illegitimate Collins! Her identity was as much a secret as ever.

Benjamin solved her problem of whether to tell the police what she'd found out or not by quietly dying that afternoon.

Then she told Elizabeth of her discovery. The attractive mistress of Collins House heard her out with mounting incredulity. At the end of the account she sank back in her chair.

"It's hard to believe," she said. "And yet I can see that it all fits. So it was Uncle Henry, and Benjamin helped him."

"But no one need ever know. Not even his son. I gather he has enough problems."

"I agree," Elizabeth said. "And I wouldn't feel guilty about the emeralds. Uncle Henry wanted you to have them because he liked you and he had a right to give them to whoever he wished." She paused. "Strangely enough, it was about all he had to bequeath anyone. He had sold all his other jewels and for some years he had been living on the proceeds of an annuity that ended with his death. His lawyer explained this when he attended the funeral. I agreed to settle any outstanding bills."

"But your uncle wouldn't have wanted that," Victoria protested. "I insist you take the emeralds and sell them to settle his estate."

In the end they came to a compromise in the matter. Elizabeth took the necklace and bracelet, with Victoria retaining the earrings as a memento of the old man.

They found a grave for Benjamin close to that of the man whom he had served faithfully all his life in his own twisted way. The two old men would be together in death as they had been during the tragic years of their lives. And when, a few days later, Jack Willard and his wife drove away from Collins House, it seemed that the strange saga of the hidden room had come to an end.

Within a few weeks the summer holidays would be over. David and Carolyn would be coming back to lighten the mood of the drab old mansion perched on that cliff by the ocean. Roger would continue in his willful ways and his drinking and Elizabeth would carry on as the dominating personality of the grim old house. In spite of her personal tragedy she would have to continue being a source of strength to the others.

Victoria and Elizabeth had finished cleaning up the apartment. Now it was in the same neat order it had been in before Henry Collins and his party arrived. Elizabeth silently led her to the door of the hidden room and they viewed it together. Then the older woman said, "I suppose there is nothing to do now but lock it up again. And permanently this time. Henry will not be back."

Sadness came over Victoria and she took a step into the high-ceilinged crimson and ivory room with its quaint old-world elegance. She said, "It's strange, but I don't feel afraid of it anymore. It doesn't seem to have that sinister evil tone it had before. Don't you notice it?"

Elizabeth frowned slightly in consideration and followed her into the room. She glanced around and then said, "You're right. There is a difference. It's so peaceful in here now. As if all the unhappy spirits were finally at rest."

Victoria said, "And it really is one of the loveliest rooms in all the house."

The older woman smiled. "You're not deceiving me for a minute. I know you're pleading its cause. And I think you've won. Why not leave it open for us all to enjoy?" Victoria's heart beat fast with happiness. She knew Henry Collins would approve. He had dreamed a dream here. If it had failed, it wasn't his fault. The dream of a true love had been right and good, as it always would be. She thought of Ernest as she went to the window. She told Elizabeth, "I'll raise this and let in some fresh air."

# Coming Soon From Hermes Press

**Book Three:** *Strangers at Collins House*
**Book Four:** *The Mystery of Collinwood*
**Book Five:** *The Curse of Collinwood*
**Book Six:** *Barnabas Collins*
**Book Seven:** *The Secret of Barnabas Collins*
**Book Eight:** *The Demon of Barnabas Collins*
**Book Nine:** *The Foe of Barnabas Collins*
**Book Ten:** *The Phantom and Barnabas Collins*
**Book Eleven:** *Barnabas Collins vs. The Warlock*
**Book Twelve:** *The Peril of Barnabas Collins*
**Book Thirteen:** *Barnabas Collins and the Mysterious Ghost*
**Book Fourteen:** *Barnabas Collins and Quentin's Demon*
**Book Fifteen:** *Barnabas Collins and the Gypsy Witch*
**Book Sixteen:** *Barnabas, Quentin and The Mummy's Curse*

...and over a dozen more thrilling *Dark Shadows* editions!

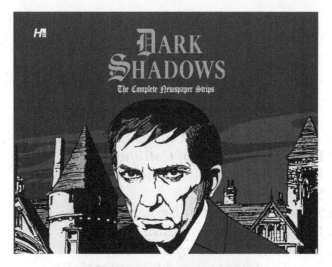
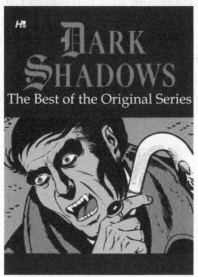